*Home & Castle*

by

Thomas Benz

**Snake~Nation~Press**
**Valdosta, Georgia   2018**

Snake Nation Press, the only independent literary press in south Georgia, publishes *Snake Nation Review*, a book of poetry by a single author each year, and a book of fiction by a single author each year. Unsolicited submissions of fiction, essays, art, and poetry are welcome throughout the year but will not be returned unless a stamped, self-addressed envelope is included. We encourage simultaneous submissions.

**Subscriptions:**
Individuals $30
Institutions $40
Foreign     $40
Sample Copy $10 (includes shipping)

Published by Snake Nation Press
110 West Force Street
Valdosta, Georgia 31601
Printed and bound in the United States of America.
Copyright © Thomas Benz 2018
All Rights Reserved

The stories in this book are works of fiction. Names, characters, places and incidents are either products of the author's imagination or are used fictitiously. Any resemblance to actual persons, living or dead, is entirely coincidental
No part of this book may be reproduced in any form, except for the quotation of brief passages, or for non-profit educational use, without prior written permission from the copyright holder.

ISBN: 978-0-9979353-2-5

*Home & Castle*

*by*

# Thomas Benz

*Snake Nation Press is a small non-profit press
dedicated to publishing literature
in all its myriad forms.
110 Force Street
Valdosta, GA 31601
www.snakenationpress.org*

# *Acknowledgements*

"A Stranger in Transit" *Paumanok Review,* Summer issue, 2004.
"Trouble with the Magi" *Carve,* Spring issue, 2005.
"Satellite View" *Willard and Maple*, 2007-2008 issue (Volume XIII).
"Casual Impostor" was the winner of the (August) 2011 *Solstice* Short Fiction Contest
"House Crawl" *Solstice,* Summer issue, 2013.
"The Protectors" *Blue Penny Quarterly,* Summer issue, 2014.
"Life Jacket" *Madison Review,* Fall/Winter, 2014 issue
"The Waiting Moon" *Mud Season Review*, Spring issue, 2017

Thomas Benz has published sixteen stories with magazines, such as *The Madison Review, William and Mary Review, the Mud Season Review, Blue Penny Quarterly, Willard and Maple, Blue Lake Review, Carve,* and others. He has written feature articles for the *Evanston Roundtable.* He won the *Solstice* Short Story Contest in 2011. He was a finalist in the *Flannery O'Connor Short Fiction Collection Contest* in 2013 and 2015. He received honorable mention in the 2014, 2015 and 2016 in *New Millennium* Short Story Contests.

At various times, he has been associated with writing organizations in the Chicago area, such as Off Campus Writers Workshop, Northwestern professor Fred Shafer's fiction workshop, the Writers Workspace, and Story Studio Chicago. He has a Bachelor's degree in English from the University of Notre Dame and a Masters Degree in Public Administration from Roosevelt University. His website is www.indielit.net.

As usual, there are a great many people to thank for supporting this long road to publication: Roberta Haas George, Jean Arambula, Pat Creevy, David Johnston, Fred Shafer and the members of his workshops, Mike Pollard, Larry Stanton, Bill Kennedy, David Dejong, David Pelzer, Paul McComas and the members of his workshops, Jacob Appel, Peter Ferry, Abby Geni, Bill Schwer, Lota Martinez, Frank O'Malley, Story Studio, Off Campus Writers Workshop, Amy Davis, my siblings and the editors of all the literary magazines in which my stories have appeared. Also, as always, I'm grateful for the considerable forbearance of my wife and son.

## *Artist's Statement*

My writing tends to gravitate toward certain themes: misunderstanding, romantic discord, the struggles of being a parent, conflict with a community's prevailing ethos, and the characters' frequent sense of exclusion from an accepted place in society. I like fictional situations where people are placed under stress, often due to their own mistakes, so that they end up reacting in a pivotal and unforeseen manner.

I enjoy the stuff of ordinary life, which, through a sequence of escalating difficulties, suddenly becomes remarkable and strange. I like depictions of the world that attempt to balance minor tragedies with irony and an occasional touch of humor. Also, the writers I most admire pay attention to the sound and rhythm of words, take risks with language and metaphor. It's wonderful when the great ones create a structure of imagery beneath the surface of a story that seems to integrate it in some mysterious way.

Much has been said about the capacity of fiction to generate empathy for other points of view and science appears to bear that out. In an era of increasing tribalism, few traits are more needed than the one which compels us to hear the other voice, feel the unusual or contradictory experience. We need not agree with different perceptions but must be able to get to the root of them before any sort of understanding can take place.

By its very nature, fiction also helps cultivate and preserve language as the primary means of apprehending the world. While the proliferation of movies and videos and photographs and emojis are a marvelous addition to our lives, only language enables the recipient to bring his or her full imagination to the encounter. A novel or collection of stories uniquely engages a reader to construct a world right along with the author, to infuse what's been created with a unique filter, to make the abstract visible in one's own mind. If a "picture is worth a thousand words," it cannot do quite the same thing as those words. In our rush to compress, to abbreviate, to go faster, to live more and more, this might be something we should not allow ourselves to forget.

## *Editors' Statement*

In *Home & Castle*, Thomas Benz as a writer does the almost impossible. He takes the ordinary and twists it just enough to make it totally original. Snake Nation Press editors in reading over 200 manuscripts have come across some really good writers. There were over 20 short-story collections in our long finalist's list for consideration this year. But Benz's writing pulled us in with that odd, original twist and the flavor of deeply insightful words and observations.

Have you ever been mistaken for another person? Of course. And, of course, you explained as quickly as possible who you were. But what if you didn't explain right away? What if you went along with the misconception, adopting that other person' identity? In "Casual Impostor," that's what the main character does, becomes the other person. Can he get away with this deception? Benz's protagonists always have that edge that makes for an interesting story, a little more courage than the average person.

Take the obvious knowledge that people often would rather see you fail, than succeed. In "Early Retirement," Benz gives us that situation in the first paragraph:

> Neal couldn't help but be annoyed when people reacted strangely to his early retirement. Their initial shock routinely gave way to shallow congratulations, and after a certain interval, the bombshell would uneasily sink in.

Giving the reader a puzzle in the first lines grabs attention. One hangs in there to see how Neal is going to work it out. Here is a man who with small economies and a lucky pick in the stock market manages to save enough to quit the nine-to-five routine. Isn't that what we all want to do? But human nature being what it is, Neal's friends and relatives cannot be happy for him. How does he resolve the problem of boredom and envy?

Lines like, "Yet there is something vaguely pleasant about being where he doesn't belong, a spy behind enemy lines." This kind of writing states the human feelings we all have had when we found ourselves in unfamiliar places. You can't stop reading the story.

Read *Home & Castle* and be that person with the edge, the courage. In fact, I, myself, want to be like the woman, Great Aunt Marian in Benz's story: "She was very old, and, in contemplation of the end, had somehow managed the demeanor of someone embarking on a cruise."

Ah, yes, when you can take wisdom like that away from a short story, you have found a treasure.

—the editors

## *Table of Contents*

Casual Impostor    9

Life Jacket    20

Early Retirement    31

Trouble with The Magi    43

The Protectors    53

The Waiting Moon    65

Last Shot at Vader    77

Home & Castle    89

Satellite View    102

A Stranger in Transit    113

House Crawl    123

## *Dedication*

*"For Ger and Evan,
two beacons in a sometimes
uncertain sea"*

## *Casual Impostor*

Though he didn't usually keep count, over the past couple years, Blake was sure he had been mistaken for someone else at least six times. Throughout his adult life, such misunderstandings had happened and lately the phenomenon seemed to have accelerated. It occurred in train stations, supermarkets, baseball stadiums, anyplace where hordes of people converged, where the odds of running into someone you recognized was exponentially increased by the numbers. It was as if there was some generic quality in his face, a kind of template that enabled people to see long-lost friends, classmates and colleagues who still generated a faint signal in the recesses of memory. He seemed to emit an invisible current that called out to strangers.

At first, he felt flattered by these episodes of confusion. It had the merest whiff of celebrity to be singled out in a crowd, to be addressed in a friendly yet tentative way by someone you had never seen before, as if you had a bit part in a small film that had just come out. There was always something marvelous in their initial expressions, thinking they had rediscovered a piece of their lives they had thought irretrievably gone. Lately though, a certain annoyance had crept into these scenarios because of the bewilderment he was beset with, as he racked his brain for some semblance in his own past. He wondered why it almost never really was him but rather some anonymous double, a hundred times more popular.

Blake recalled that one time he had retreated from a lacerating February wind inside a café, where he waited for the university bus. It was a good spot because there was a kind of alcove where he could be separated from the actual customers, and without paying a cent, he could loiter and take in the rich atmosphere of the coffee. His mind mostly wandered to the mountains of files awaiting him at his desk, a permanent backlog not of his own doing, that properly could have been one of the seven labors of Hercules.

"Lester?" the man there had almost whispered, leaning in suddenly. He was massive and completely bald, with those odd uneven surfaces everyone conceals beneath their hair. This guy was so sure of his errant recognition, he put his arm around Blake's shoulder before asking him if his handicap was still four. Never so much as having touched a golf club in his life, and never being greatly enamored with hugs even among his few friends, Blake was nonplussed. He shook him off as if reacting to an assault, which of course wrecked the man's generous smile in an instant and had him backpedaling with his hands raised in a universal sign of surrender.

Ever since these strange encounters began happening in his early twenties, he wondered if he should he act as if he were unfazed or shocked, as if the interlocutor had just escaped from an asylum. "No, I'm sorry," was Blake's more customary reply. He usually let them down easy so that the impact of their blunders wouldn't hit them full force. Eventually he settled into a kind of benign condescension, as he was the one being accosted, the one armed with the true circumstances. It was nothing high handed, just enough to preserve some sense of personal space like a country that claims a couple miles of territorial water.

Another time it happened at the airport. He and Chloe were headed out to a couples spa in Palm Springs for a desperately needed vacation. They had paraded through the two-hour security ordeal and were waiting to board. They were sitting in the concourse with their exorbitantly priced cinnamon rolls watching planes with different brands and markings taxi along the endless expanses of runway. A well-dressed man looking to be about Blake's age came toward them with the ubiquitous luggage on wheels, his eyes fixed as if trying to read some inscription on Blake's forehead.

"Jim, where have you been hiding?" he blurted, as Chloe coughed in response to this ambush. It may have been worse this time either because Chloe was present or due to the fact that they were sitting down, which lent the effect of being pinned in a corner. Blake took a second to swallow the last of his hasty breakfast and gather some composure.

"Nowhere . . . ," he said evenly. "Maybe it's you who's been so scarce." His identity was being stolen in little increments every time he was figured for someone else, and now he was getting even, restoring the yin and yang. Chloe gave him a shaken look, as if he had a nickname he had never divulged to her, a secret compartment to his life. The man didn't quite know what to make of this ambiguous remark, whether it was a real charge of abandonment or merely the usual male jousting. "I can't believe it. You haven't changed…" was all he could come up with in response. For a few seconds Blake considered letting this go another round, but Chloe's anxious glances were bearing down on him like a physical pressure and he relented.

As the people around them began to rise at the announcement for boarding passes, he said, "I'm sorry, there's been some mix-up. I'm not Jim."

He pulled the driver's license from his wallet to demonstrate he wasn't kidding. Blake felt a certain duty to relieve the guy's embarrassment after having played along and callously holding his misjudgment in suspense. "Don't feel bad," Blake went on. "This happens to me pretty often. I must have one of those everyman faces."

When the man shrugged and then ambled off in search of his gate, Chloe turned to Blake and said, "What exactly was that?"

"I'm not sure. But it's like being some poor soul in a police lineup where the victim is half blind."

Later, once they had reached cruising altitude, Blake thought about how exhilarating it had been perpetuating the illusion for a while, the rush of slyly entering another life. If it was a rather cruel game, he wasn't the one who had invited it. He wondered if that might be the key to breaking the curse, to ending the cycle of his somehow being dozens of people whose uniqueness was so fuzzy as to be virtually nonexistent. As he peered down at the aerial clarity of the earth, it suddenly seemed perfectly legitimate to be a casual impostor, not in an attempt to crash some high society ball or a nuclear facility but just for the experience of being someone else for a time, someone he didn't even know.

During those same few months, Chloe began offering accounts of a recurring dream with an almost feverish persistence. The reveries had him conducting a coldly calculated affair with Chloe's friend, Megha, and her descriptions were nearly cinematic in their vividness. They told her the motels where the liaisons occurred, the perfume and type of shoes Megha was wearing, the elaborate fiction Blake had concocted about his whereabouts, even the brand of cabernet they sipped as they lay naked beside one another.

Naturally, he and Chloe had laughed at the beginning but after a while it became like a lurid soap opera. If Blake got up to find something else to do in the middle of another installment, she would follow him around the house, seeming to remember more outlandish aspects of the dream as she uttered them. It was yet another subversion of his real identity, not only because he was depicted as a rakish player in her unconscious but because on some subtle level, she seemed to be judging him on the basis of these nightly scandals. It was nothing she would come out and say, outwardly at least. Chloe was had always been certain he was beyond reproach and that no other woman would be interested enough to chase him. Rather the very idea seemed to create an inner disturbance, a withdrawal in her manner that he could trace to no other cause.

What made matters worse was that Megha was lovely—the chestnut eyes and narrow waist, the general insouciance—and he had long nurtured a kind of never to be fulfilled crush. She would jog through the neighborhood in her sweatpants or demure shorts, her agile figure still somehow limned inside the loose fabric. Her breathing never seemed strained, as she had been a cross-country athlete in her college days. In the course of his weekend errands, Blake had spotted her a couple times, but she had been so ensconced, both in the rhythm of her exertion and the insulated auditory world of her headphones, that he hadn't even tried to say hello. He had just watched the feline grace of her movement until she became obscured by traffic or merely drifted beyond a row of townhouses.

Only one moment at a party long ago had he ever really been tempted. She and her obtuse husband Rudy were leaving, and Blake went to retrieve her jacket, strewn in a heap with the others in the dark bedroom, Megha leading the way. Blake supposed he didn't think to turn on the light because he was half drunk, and it took her a half minute of rummaging to find it. Of course, there was something electric about her search in the dusky room and when she caught a heel and started to fall, he reflexively caught her with the result that his face sank into her soft neck for the brief interval it took to regain their balance.

They both withdrew from the unwitting embrace, though as they went back out there was none of the embarrassed laughter he had expected, but instead the silence of an implicit exchange. Blake felt it was not in his DNA to have an affair with anyone, that such a betrayal would stalk his conscience like a predator, yet Chloe's accounts of his nonexistent infidelity had stirred something there, amid the stack of coats. Afterward, the imprint of that happy accident became as indelible as his own countenance.

One night Chloe informed him that Megha and Rudy were getting a divorce. Megha had come over that afternoon while he was at work, spilling the story. Having been married six years, she had accumulated several reasons, but it was Rudy who kept accusing Megha of acting strangely, of aloofness, of creating rancor. She had gone by the time Blake got home, but sitting in a favorite leather chair in the living room, he seemed to detect a hint of whatever scent she had been wearing. Chloe and Megha were on the phone a lot the next few weeks, and one afternoon in another room Blake picked up the receiver, not realizing they were on the line.

Megha was lightly crying in that sniffling way that makes the sound almost indistinguishable from a cold or an allergy. In the few seconds he eavesdropped, he instinctively wanted to console her, just as he had caught her before she hurtled toward the pointed corner of a bookcase in their bedroom. He might have diverted her with the many fun outings the three of them had had together when her husband was roaming the country on business: Yo Yo Ma in the park at Ravinia, the lakeboat cruise where they were all as high as a hot air balloon, and the occasional baseball game in the bleachers. But he softly put the phone down on the dresser and scurried out to the garage.

At some point during the gray doldrums of winter, Chloe began to stare when he would be watching TV or reading *National Geographic*, as if she were focusing some occult beam that rummaged through the locked compartments of his psyche. She would probe Blake's itineraries and scrutinize the timelines of his absences like a detective on one of the dozens of dreary cop shows that now littered the airwaves. On one occasion, she examined a vaguely horizontal sauce stain on his collar and said, "Interesting shade of lipstick" before tossing the shirt listlessly into the hamper. He became resentful of this surveillance, even more because it had no legitimate basis. Beyond such needless spying, Chloe's romantic attentions dwindled, no doubt the consequence of getting a crash course in all of Rudy's vices and inconsiderateness. She began spending more time with her animal rights group, which appeared to regard humans as a heartless and vastly inferior species.

For a while, Blake had walked the streets and gone to bars and movies without being hailed by some misbegotten passerby with incipient myopia or cataracts. There were a few inevitable instances when he would bump into people he did know but not very well, and he noticed during the inevitable small talk a certain defensiveness, as if they too might be mistaken somehow. Still, before the incident with Renfield, the whole doppelganger phenomenon seemed to be receding like some aberrant chapter in adolescence that vanishes without a trace.

One Thursday, Blake was having souvlaki in Plato's, a Greek restaurant only a few blocks from work but a spot where he had seldom ventured, owing to the medieval strictures of his lunch break. It was one of those places with murals of terraced cities along the Adriatic coast and frescoes of the retinue of Mount Olympus, with their lyres and thunderbolts. A fleeting warm front had drifted in, and the bosses were at a conference, so he was determined to eat with some leisure for a change.

"Paul, is it really you?" came a voice at the edge of his solitary table. There had been something different about this one, some almost desperate timbre that this Paul be found again at last. The man seemed in a kind of daze, hesitant, non-threatening. Blake detected a certain kindness in his dull eyes, and was seized with the complicated impulse to both befriend and deceive an errant stranger that had first struck at the airport.

"Who else would it be? Great to see you." The rejoinder came so naturally this time, as if he were filming a scene that he had rehearsed for days, settling on a few nuances and discarding others that had felt contrived. Finishing the last of his olives, Blake had the sense to proceed slowly and allow the details to be laid out before him. If he were to be exposed, he would plead some kind of minor mental illness, and if that didn't work, it crossed his mind that the skewers that ran through the columns of meat could be brandished in self-defense.

"Has it really been fourteen years since Columbus?" the gentleman said, his ears still flushed with surprise, as the disbelief at the edge of his smile began to recede.

"Sad but true. *Tempus fugit*. I didn't even know you were living here," Blake said, with the veneer of a barely muted enthusiasm.

"Me either. We moved a year and a half ago. A job I just couldn't pass up. Son of a bitch. There's something different about you."

"You're not exactly a carbon copy yourself," Blake replied evenly. "But you look good. I would have recognized you anywhere."

The man sat down almost in slow motion, laying his laptop case on the floor. "You still on the tax side of things?"

"No. I switched a few years back. That's probably how we lost touch."

Blake felt strangely relaxed, sensing he would somehow be able to navigate through the minefield of ruses, eliciting information about his double's past as he went along. There was one moment when he thought he would surely be unmasked as a fraud, but it passed quickly with a change of subject.

The fellow diner's name was Ned Renfield, father of four and supposed alumnus of Ohio State. Ned was an avid member of Facebook and mentioned a number of of their mutual friends, giving him a thumbnail sketch of their situations. Fortunately, there had been no sudden deaths to report, just the usual half- life woes of marriages gone bad, minor scrapes with the law, and career fiascos.

"It's funny how things turn out. Emmett had his wild side, but I would have thought him headed for big things, a CEO or something," Renfield said, after describing how their old buddy had recently gone down in flames amid a securities scandal. "I'm surprised you haven't heard from him, Paul. You were pretty close."

"It's terrible, I know. I just can't keep all the balls in the air lately."

"Do you remember when he broke into the provost's office?" Ned blurted, carried back by the memory.

"God, he had nerves of steel."

"That's the way we all were back then. No regard for the consequences. What was it that he took? You were there, with the getaway car so to speak."

Even then, Blake didn't so much panic as feel a twinge of excitement. They were both just actors trying to get the emotions right–the director could yell cut at any moment and they could start all over. Still, he sensed the merest tremor traveling up his left side, as Ned watched him with the fond anticipation of reminiscence.

"How can I not remember that?" Blake lightly knocked his temple with the heel of his hand, as if to jog the nonexistent information free. "I really ought to cut down on my drinking."

Blake hoped that might get a chuckle and create an opportunity for a segue but it didn't shake Ned's intentness. There were a few seconds where Ned was perfectly still, not even blinking while Blake braced himself for the dreaded scene, the incredulity and contorted expressions, the hard stares from waiters and other patrons.

"The bookends!" Renfield half shouted, drawing a few glances. "Egyptian Figures. Sphinxes, that's what they were."

"Of course," Blake recovered, then felt his confidence coming back like a burst of oxygen. "The provost acted like they were solid gold."

"It's a good thing Emmett was able to get them back the next night."

"Yes, a prank instead of grand larceny."

"Maybe it was just a matter of time with him. That the one would turn into the other. . . ," Renfield said.

While Blake considered whether to probe this directly, Renfield looked at his watch and got to his feet, explaining that he was already late for a meeting, and handed Blake his business card. He made him promise to call so they could catch up some more.

"This is so terrific," Ned gushed, looking back, as he started to make his way out. "I thought I had lost the trail."

There was another party, Herb Harbin's annual April Fools gala, which had become a rite of spring. It featured a number of objects scattered in plain sight throughout the house that were somehow counterfeit. He offered a prize for the one who could identify the most. In past years, there had been fake diplomas, cigarettes that would not light, forged books, clocks that ran backwards, and sundry other hoaxes. According to Chloe, Megha was supposed to be there, and Blake mused about seeing her without the hulking presence of Rudy whose gravity always threw her into a slightly different orbit. When Chloe came down with a nasty chest cold, it caught him off guard that she insisted he go anyway. Maybe this was a test, and she had spies planted in every alcove, or perhaps the coughing and chills had caused the Megha factor to slip her mind.

He had not seen her since the break-up, and she wasn't yet there when he arrived. As he navigated the house for bogus items, Blake sifted through the different ways he could act: empathetic, pretending nothing had happened, playing up the supposed gaiety of the occasion to help her forget her Neanderthal lover. He wondered if she might exhibit any detectible change from the separation, some ineffable mark of loss that made her even more beautiful. But he didn't entertain the idea that he was any more a part of her universe than he ever had been and just wanted to soothe her whatever way he could.

Just as Blake decided she wasn't coming and even the real objects in Harbin's home began to seem fake in a terrible way, Megha was suddenly there at the edge of the cramped kitchen, dressed down in faded jeans and an oversized pastel shirt. She leaned against a wall in a languid manner, lending the appearance of a woman so fragile, as to barely remain upright.

Blake didn't want to interrupt her conversation with Lila, a friend of Chloe's he'd never much liked, but then Megha wandered over by the fireplace. She nodded as he approached but looked a bit lost, her eyes appearing uncharacteristically vacant, as if she had gotten a considerable head start on the alcohol.

"I heard about poor Chloe," she said, smiling wanly to help free him from the guilt of deserting her.

"Yeah, she practically kicked me out the door," he said, and immediately regretted his choice of words. "In her case, misery doesn't love company."

"Have you found any of Herb's hidden tricks yet?"

"Only a little funny money—George Bush's mug smack in the middle. He'll be lucky to get his own stamp."

"Well, you better try harder," she said, with a hint of that Punjabi accent that was like a beguiling spice in an unusual dish you couldn't quite label. "You're never going to win the grand prize." Her head sagged a little when she spoke as if the weight of it were too much to lift upright, and kept one hand against the mantel. She didn't appear sad so much as stranded somehow, on the side of some country road. Blake rummaged through a collection of safe topics, but they all sounded stilted to him somehow.

He dearly wanted to confide about the Renfield incident, so strange he had not even entrusted it to Chloe. Blake thought that somehow in her broken condition she would understand why it had been so cathartic to impersonate someone else for a while. But in the end, he held back because he feared the story might have the wrong effect, make her feel more jaded and unmoored than she already did. Megha turned to scan the other guests, perhaps as a prelude to escape, revealing the elegant curve of her neck again, with a spray of curls symmetrically falling around it. The angle of her profile reminded him of a sculpture he had seen but couldn't remember where.

"There's a Kilhoff exhibit coming to the Institute," he said quickly to fix her there a moment longer. "Some very nice stuff. Reminds me a little of Hopper, the urban landscapes, the people in the middle of something, but you can't figure out quite what."

"Yes, I saw a couple of his paintings at the Metropolitan. Really interesting," she said, momentarily emerging from her fog, just as shouts arose from the den where Lila had stumbled across a revolver that shot bubbles. "We should go some time," she said in a voice that immediately seemed slight and wounded, containing the notes of all that had happened.

"Yes, we should," Blake said with a little hesitance, unable to keep from exploring the ambiguity about whether 'we' included his slumbering wife. "I'll find out when it is."

Just then, Wendell Ross, one of the neighbors they hardly knew, tripped rounding a couch too quickly, sprawling at the foot of a mammoth antique bureau. By the time Blake and a couple others helped him up and retrieved his miraculously unbroken glass, Megha had fled to the other side of the house and must have slipped out the back door.

The last time Blake met Ned was on a Saturday, a few miles east of where he and Chloe lived. He wasn't going to let him get too close to his real life, with all the preparation that would entail, but Quincy's was the only place in that direction he could think of when Renfield again contacted him out of the blue. Quincy's was an old fashioned tavern Blake had repaired to on many occasions when his own set of walls became oppressive, one that had not succumbed to the craze for ubiquitous flat screen TV's.

Blake had slowly become fascinated with his new persona, the cavalier, fun-loving adventurer he was never destined to be. He recalled a few of the enticements he'd passed up over the years due to some excess financial or moral scruple. The trips to South America Chet Rittenaur took every January, the marijuana trances Bob Gooley still engaged in with their pals on his patio, and the excursions to strip clubs that a different crowd scheduled with an almost liturgical frequency. Blake's demurrals had always shunted him to the periphery of every group, this dull reluctance to take the blind leap.

He joined Ned at a weathered wooden booth by the bar. Maybe it was the early afternoon hour, but some of the spark of their initial meetings had dissipated. For a while, Blake was glad to put the ball in Ned's court, pepper Renfield with questions so that he could give the lying center in his brain a break, rest on the fabrications he had already made. After some small talk, Renfield showed him pictures of his kids, told him that his wife Alise had recently broken her ankle, that there was something messed up with the insurance. Maybe that was what was spooking Ned that day, that things had changed, that the aura of college could only carry them so far.

"It just occurred to me I haven't seen you smoking," Ned interjected at one point, looking almost shocked at the absence of a Marlboro or Lucky Strike wedged between Blake's fingers.

"Yes, one demon down, several more to go."

"By the way, how's Madeleine? I've been dying to ask."

"Not sure. She's in a land far, far away," Blake said, with what he hoped would pass for amused resignation.

"You're kidding. I'm sorry," Renfield said, concerned enough that Blake had to dial his mood down a notch.

"It's okay. *C'est la vie.*"

"So you're with someone else?"

"Well, yes. Though it hasn't been that long. We'll see if the cure will take."

There was a sense that Ned's inquiries were coming a bit too fast, that the exhilaration of making things up was starting to make him feel a touch dizzy, but it was all still under control. Blake had a brief interior glimpse of Chloe with her temperament lately like unpredictable weather—global cooling perhaps. Her image flickered back and forth conflicting with that of Paul's Madeleine whose features, wholly imagined, refused to coalesce.

"I can't imagine you without Madeleine. I never saw two people so happy. You were like the royal couple," Ned said, his scratchy voice trailing off at the end. "Something in me doesn't want to believe it."

Blake noticed that Renfield seemed distracted, a little distant perhaps, as he absorbed each new piece of incongruous background on his old pal.

"It took a while for me, too," Blake said, searching for a way to pivot into more familiar territory.

"How did you mess that up, Paul?" Ned tried to smile when he said it but the muscles around his mouth wouldn't hold, so that the remark became tinged with accusation.

Blake ran through the series of scenarios he had considered when the inevitable topic of his love life came up, but none of them seemed to appeal to him anymore. They all triggered some strange melancholy that made the subterfuge suddenly like lifting a hundred pounds of dead weight, like inheriting someone else's sins.

"An affair, what else? Nothing very original." As Blake said this, he found himself scrambling for the next move. He hit upon a few of the details he recalled from Chloe's dreams: a green slit skirt, an impetuous trip to the Florida Keys, the curious seduction of stealth itself.

"Oh, well. It happens, I guess." Renfield said, pronouncing his tepid forgiveness when none had been asked for. "You do what you have to do."

Then Ned got a call, the ring a Miles Davis or Bill Evans tune from decades ago. He had to pick up his teenager from band practice because a friend's ride had inexplicably fallen through. He apologized with the harried deportment of a father constantly in demand. But Blake thought he detected a hint of relief as well, a slow disappointment that had been seeping into Renfield's take on the new version of Paul. In a split second, Blake knew he had taken the game too far. He was flooded with a kind of latent regret, as if he had stolen an object of great value and later would have to confess, so as to restore everything that Paul might still have become.

They lingered for a moment outside the place under the awning, saying their goodbyes, suggesting tenuous plans. Just as Ned turned a bit abruptly and ambled toward his car, Blake saw Megha jogging by wearing the sunglasses and blue ski cap she still needed as winter failed to relinquish its grip, her breath condensing in the frigid air like an apparition. He figured he should at least wave, as if this were shorthand for the fact that he had decided to call her about the Kilhoff exhibit. It seemed the easiest thing in the world now, and Chloe would never be interested, because people lived in different worlds that only intersected occasionally and mostly by chance. The distance was too great for his voice to carry, so he extended his arm as if he was reaching for something, letting it sway rhythmically like a semaphore. She stopped in mid stride, still pumping her legs in the simulation of movement, struggling to recognize him through the glare of the street. After several seconds of peering across the thoroughfare, an unreadable look spread across the contours of her face. Megha couldn't be sure, must not have known who he was, as she turned and began moving farther and farther away.

## *Life Jacket*

Brett knows the routine by now as they arrive at Tuttle Park, gathering an assortment of balls, mitts, and a Frisbee out of the trunk, though odds are he has lugged them out here for nothing. He knows Charlie loves him, but that as an only child, his son craves the company of other kids. Brett may be able to extort ten minutes of dad time at the end when they're already late for dinner, risking Holly's ire for pushing the whole bed schedule further into the night. When they reach the entrance, Charlie is like a thoroughbred springing out of the gate at Arlington, as he races toward the massive wooden structure that draws him here. There is no playground like it: a cave, castle, fort, tunnel network and gauntlet all rolled into one. Its sprawling warren most resembles some manmade reef set down on the edge of a field, small elusive creatures darting in and out. Charlie scales a hidden stairway and manages to join a group of chasing boys, tags along as seamlessly as a pickpocket slips through a crowd.

Brett drops the jumble of sports equipment next to one of the picnic tables. Tuttle Park has always vexed him because every view seems to be obstructed, and his six-year-old is always disappearing in its catacombs. It bothers Brett less than it used to, but he is still spooked by the myriad tragedies he runs across in the newspapers—people get killed on golf courses, disappear into sinkholes, perish in their own beds when a twin-engine Cessna plummets out of the sky. Especially with children, accidents seem to lurk everywhere and require a constant vigilance. Charlie's wearing a purple sweatshirt that says *Mischief University*, and flashes of this insignia are the only way to follow his movements. Even so, amid all the hiding places, it would be easier to track a rare bird in the wild.

Brett should be reading a report from work, but he left it in the backseat and can't bring himself to mar such a buoyant scene with its dreary analysis. The other assembled caretakers are distracting themselves on the internet, but his phone is so antiquated, it barely serves the function of transporting a voice. He is still carrying the book on Atlantis Charlie insisted on bringing along, but having read the story a dozen times now, no amount of boredom could induce Brett to open it. The same goes for Charlie's other favorite *Oog and Gloog,* which features cavemen continually getting into some primitive trouble.

The way things have been going lately, Brett needs some diversion to keep unpleasant thoughts from appearing out of nowhere. He'd rather not wait for all the little episodes to return in slow-motion replay, an exchange gone awry or some mishap that might easily have been prevented. He has only to recapitulate the last couple months to find a whole raft of these. An "inappropriate" email got sent to the wrong person resulting in, at best, a terrible misunderstanding. Then, there was his collision with Claire Parnell, after having charged out of his cubicle like a rhino, and the *coup de gras,* a glaring error he made in a brochure that couldn't be called back in time. Brett Hanbeck once again in a predicament of his own making.

It is an early autumn afternoon in Milwaukee where that sweet season won't last long. The air is warm in the sun and chilly in the shade, so that by turns Brett feels over and underdressed. Feathery leaves, not yet brittle, lose their moorings and float down from the branches. There is some tune playing faintly out in the streets that seems to shift with the wind. Brett gets a call, the ring jarring, too much like the insistence of a mild shock. He considers dodging it, but seeing Holly's number on the display, he jabs the answer button. "I have some bad news," she prefaces the conversation. He has asked her never to begin this way, that to do so generally conjures up trouble far worse than whatever she has to express. But she keeps doing it anyway, feeling this intro will soften the message's impact, allow him to gradually process the disappointment, and keep his circuits from blowing a fuse.

"The car needs a new transmission," she says, keeping her voice even, perhaps trying to mimic the harmless delivery of the mechanic, whose manner is as soothing as a social worker. The sound they've been hearing isn't just the fuel pump, which makes sense since the beast has 114 thousand miles on it by now. The last year or so, Brett has kept his eye on the Sonata, nursing it along, knowing it can't last forever. Any real fix will be a grand at least, and they're still trying to claw their way back from the nose-dive of real estate prices, the mortgage underwater.

"Should we have them do it or . . .?"

He knows what the "or" is—a brand new vehicle that would be suicide in the middle of a recession—so he cuts her off. "I think so, but get a firm estimate first. Don't let him bamboozle you."

"He's a good guy, Brett. You know that."

He thinks she's solicitous of the mechanic because he looks like Mark Wahlberg, an actor she finds attractive in some stoic, musclebound way.

He tries to go easy on the small stuff because Holly is a saint who has finessed them through a hundred squabbles. She's given to late-night crime show binging, but is otherwise admirably restrained. Still, she seems to be wearing down, last night suggesting that he deliberately sabotaged himself so he'd be fired. It's well known what he thinks of Croyden Marketing, one step up from a coal mine–maybe. But without other prospects and a load of debt, he wasn't about to do anything rash.

"Okay honey, thanks for the doomsday update," Brett says. "We'll be back pretty soon."

He has come to the park so often lately, he can't help studying the cover of Charlie's first-grade book just to escape Tuttle's provincial boundaries. The illustration convincingly depicts a charming kingdom beneath the waves. Atlantis is a subject of fascination to Charlie and as real as the Trader Joe's at the end of their block. There's a part in the first chapter about Poseidon's assistant not being sure if she should offer up the last key to the magnificent city. She warns that while the palace is made of gold, it is also a ghost town, a figment of the irretrievable past.

Charlie sticks his head up through one of the apertures, alighting on a shaky platform, and shouts some code to his new mates. He is too skinny, would rather do almost anything than eat, his shoulder blades bulging in the shape of harps. He's always finding a refuge and combining disparate objects in unusual ways, creating his own chimera. Brett thinks he must feel protected in the maze, immune to all that confronts him outside, sheltered in the cocoon of his own imagination. Charlie has a game where he pretends everything is submerged and everyone is traipsing around the ocean floor.

"What happens if you have trouble making it to Atlantis?" Brett calls out. "The water is rough or something. What do you do then?"

"You wear a life jacket, Dad," Charlie says dismissively, before vanishing again.

Brett picks a secluded spot where he can avert one of those "we're all in the same boat" exchanges. He has had enough of them at baseball games and soccer practices to last a lifetime. Like his own father, he knows he doesn't have the knack for offhand banter and is always struggling to navigate the shoals of incidental relationship. The casual camaraderie he often sees elsewhere doesn't seem to reach him, as if he's somehow on another island. Brett certainly senses this discord with his boss Rex Yader, who never gives him a break and only seems to notice when something goes awry.

Brett glimpses Sara Chang over on the far end near the giant sandbox. She's a little overweight, but pretty, with a face that always seems somehow soft and composed. He has only talked to her a handful of times, chance encounters in the community house where many of the after-hours workshops take place. She doesn't notice him, despite his having caught her daughter Michelle maybe three years before, practically in self-defense, as she plunged head first from the high slide at another playground. If he had been a foot farther away, he probably would have frozen, but being almost directly underneath, it was like some acrobatic act they had practiced over and over.

Lost in the tense memory of this, Brett gets blindsided by Monica Wilkins, another woman from the neighborhood who has quietly entered the park, son Curtis in tow, with all the stealth of an assassin. He remembers that Holly knows her a little and that they all talked at Revere Elementary's Sea Animal Night. The early grades there seem inordinately focused on the sea. Charlie can probably name more amphibians than Brett and describe what they like to eat. There are field trips to the aquarium; drawings of whales and dolphins stretch endlessly along the school walls.

Monica is only feet away, and without any props at her disposal, feels compelled to wander in his direction. She produces a semblance of a smile he would bet exceeds his own earnest attempt. She's wearing a loose jumper that seems like it belongs somewhere closer to a barn, but she pulls it off, still looking faintly sexy.

"Where's Charlie?"

"Somewhere between the jail and drawbridge, I think" he says, gesturing vaguely toward one section of the labyrinth. A lot of adults seem to know Charlie because he's so outgoing. At church, he walks the length of the pew for the sign of peace, shaking hands as if he's running for alderman. This confidence delights Brett whose nickname was "Hang Back" in grade school, which morphed into "Hammock" in college—an image he tended to cultivate, though it was probably misleading.

"How's he liking Revere?" she asks, watching Curtis's tentative pass at a climbing wall.

"So far so good. No charges of assault and battery yet," he says, raising his eyebrows.

Monica visibly frowns before processing this crass comment as a weak attempt at humor. "Curtis still seems to be in a bit of a transition phase," she says, looking down and grabbing her neck like she has a sudden knot in it. "But he can count to five hundred."

"Now there's a skill you can use in real life," Brett says reflexively with a sarcasm he didn't intend. He knows never to make a joke concerning somebody else's kid if there's even a chance this could be taken the wrong way and wishes he could retract it, as in a court proceeding where a statement can be stricken from the record.

Monica's cheeks tighten in a way that makes clear she wishes she were someplace else, anyplace else. She thrusts her hand deep into a cavernous shoulder bag in search of a gadget that won't insult her, and in profile says, "Got to go."

"Hope to see you at Fallfest," he says, overcompensating for his tactlessness. The fact is he dearly wishes to avoid that annual event, with its bedlam of exhibits and awful bands. The teachers are already leery because he doesn't have time to volunteer. Everyone else seems to know each other from food drives and benefits. So when he is marooned at one of those functions, at some point he invariably begins to feel as if the planet's oxygen is running out. Sea Animal Night was the exception because Charlie had a brief dance number, and Brett couldn't resist seeing his son up on stage as a starfish in some Vaudeville sketch.

"Little help here," Charlie cries out, his voice a mixture of frustration, embarrassment, and perhaps a tinge of anxiety.

Brett can't discern if there's an actual danger or if this is another in Charlie's repertoire of antics. Jumping up, he sees Charlie's gotten snared, trying to squeeze through one of the tight spaces, seeking a path that wasn't there. He's pulling against some kind of spoked wheel, and his reaction to being rendered stationary is tense but unafraid. Brett extracts him with some repositioning of limbs and tugs of fabric. Released, Charlie is all exuberance again, the whole thing instantly forgotten.

"Are we still going to Six Flags?" Charlie asks. "That boy said he went last weekend and it was the best day he ever had."

"That one got by us, pal. They're closed now. We'll do it next year for sure."

Charlie shoots his father a sullen look, as if he would turn him to stone if he could. Brett's come to believe that with kids it's just truth or lies, absent any shading or nuance. Brett will take him to Six Flags next summer. He wanted to wait one more year so Charlie might still remember it when he gets to be Brett's age. Being the youngest sibling, Brett's recollection of the Enchanted Forest, the amusement park of his youth, is pleasant but hazy. Talking trees, hawkers dressed as elves, the arabesque coasters, carny booths and winding trails, the rolls of tickets and cascading bulbs. He's heard the place isn't like that anymore, the carnivals having been sterilized by huge corporations. But now he feels bad that he didn't do Six Flags this year because Charlie is transfixed with the idea and somehow sons are always judging their fathers even after they're gone. Brett still has a few issues with his own, though he has come to feel his dad did as well as he could, given the regular onslaughts from everywhere. So what if he liked the casino, the track, and the Early Times a bit too much. Even if it left you feeling untethered for certain stretches, who would fault him now?

Brett returns to his bench and finally takes out the extra hotdog from their customary stop at Henderson's Last Stand before heading to the park. The resident squirrel he's heard the kids calling Shim-Shim is rummaging for acorns to put in his hibernation savings account. He bets the twitchy creature doesn't have a fraction of what he needs to carry him through the winter, just as Brett has no surplus stash for the property taxes due in January, right when the Christmas bills start rolling in. Shim-shim's as tame and bold as a pan handler, edging up within inches of his foot. Brett feels some kinship and tosses him a big hunk of the bun. But this impulse sets off a chain reaction in the overstuffed onions and tomatoes and mustard so that they cascade down and and smear the logo of his shirt. His temper flares as it does once in a while, rising out of some unseen combination of elements like a summer squall. But he tamps down the charge before it can fully release and merely swears under his breath.

"No good deed goes unpunished, right, Shim-shim?" Brett says, rubbing his chest back and forth to blot out the stain.

Considering how the day is going and the dicey situation at work, Brett wishes he had thought to bring a Xanax, wishes there was a service for that drug like delivering a pizza. It's more discreet than a pint of whiskey, yet he'd settle for that relief now, too, regardless of the killer looks he'd get if someone spotted him. Bourbon was his father's antidote for PTSD from Korea, done with a flask, a nice one to give it the veneer of respectability. But he had weathered that experience for a long time, and it was only after his father was cut loose from the real estate firm late in his career, over nothing really, some invented infraction to improve the bottom line, that he began to slide. He would drink and hum a dance hall song to himself—Brett doesn't recall the words exactly—probably something from better days. It was like a wall went up, and you couldn't get through and you couldn't reach him. He might as well have been on the other side of the moon.

One of the other parents yells, "No head butting Walter!" and the child retreats, chastened by the public rebuke. Brett takes out his wallet, a hodgepodge of worn compartments. He starts stripping it of the detritus of old matters: a ballgame ticket stub, an expired beach pass, business cards with messages and names he barely recognizes. Then he feels the angel coin that came with some charity solicitation, and it falls out of one of the pockets into his lap. Brett's lucky if he gets to mass once a month anymore, but he's as superstitious as a fortune-teller. Something in the profile of the piece, an introspective gaze perhaps, always seemed to suggest a reluctant angel. It suddenly reminds him of the figure in the Atlantis book who is unsure whether the situation is serious enough to intervene.

Brett scans the hill at the east edge of the park, so isolated it could be an ancient burial mound, with a chamber Tuttle secretly kept for himself. He wants to leave now but knows he must give Charlie advance notice or he will protest all the way home. "Five minutes, Charlie," he signals, displaying that many fingers, though that is only an opening bid.

"Dad, watch this. I'm doing it," Charlie screams, calling him to be witness to his first complete passage across the ascending monkey bars, a move that has so far defeated him on every attempt. Brett doesn't have time to put the wallet back together properly, just mashing what he wants to keep into the main fold. He needs to get there, not for a picture he doesn't have the equipment to take, but just to see this trick, fix the impression in his mind so that it might crowd out a few of the less pleasant ones. He begins jogging rapidly through the obstacle course, knowing there is only so much strength in Charlie's arms, and he doesn't want to ruin his chances. There is no time to go around the wobbly bridge, the rocking horse, or the spherical column he stoops through, keeping his eyes fixed on Charlie, who is suspended in mid-air straining for the last rung.

"Dad, where are you?"

"I got you, buddy. It's awesome."

Climbing through one last barrier, Brett turns a fraction too much, so that the angle of the sun becomes like a laser, blinding him for the two seconds it takes to render a steel bar completely invisible. He walks right into it, striking his lower forehead with enough force to send him reeling and blinking back stars. It's a small miracle he doesn't bellow a reflexive curse that would be absorbed by so many innocent ears. Dumfounded, he merely crotches down, making sure his skull is intact.

"You okay, Dad?" Charlie asks, now on the ground.

Brett checks to see if his nose is broken, but there is only a welt rising angrily at its base. The pain has migrated diffusely from lobe to lobe but it is manageable. Only a couple of adults appear to be staring his way with bemused expressions. Brett suppresses the urge to lash out at Charlie, ask him why he's always calling him to watch some mundane performance that every other kid on the block can do. But he's vowed never to take his frustrations out on his son just because everything else seems to be spiraling out of control.

"Yeah champ. Just a little goof up." He immediately regrets using that term because it was exactly what his boss threw at him about the typesetting glitch. Of course, the way Yader said it made the oversight sound like Brett had pressed the wrong button at a nuclear missile post. On top of that, Rex set up some mysterious meeting for next week with one of the bigwigs, and Brett can't stop wondering what it's about.

"You just need better glasses, maybe?" Charlie says, trying to hand him an excuse.

Brett takes off his useless, mangled shades, which now slant diagonally across his temples. Then, the ice cream truck sidles up to the curb in the vicinity of the see-saw, playing the stale chorus of an old jingle he can't place. Children flock to the sound, under the spell of its uncanny allure.

"I bet ice cream would make you feel better," Charlie says, timidly attempting to turn the incident in his favor.

Brett recognizes this as a line he's used himself, when his son has become inconsolable about something that didn't go his way. "Did you make it, Charlie? All the way to the top?" Brett asks, shooting a daggered look at the now apparent beam that whacked him.

"I thought I was going to fall, but then I got some super strength. Didn't you see?"

They walk over to where there's a line already twisting away from the van. Brett has grabbed the football on the way, hoping to coax Charlie to play catch after the bribe has been carried out. The transactions ahead in the queue are halting, but for once Charlie has his mind set. He wants the Ironman one in the shape of the hero himself, outlined in colored ice.

The Good Humor truck plays the maddeningly simple melody again and again. Brett can't fathom why these vendors always use such archaic songs. He thinks they would have changed them to hip-hop by now, but perhaps there is something hypnotic in those notes and their sprightly cadence—the pied piper returning for an encore. Brett's pretty sure it's the same song they used when he was a kid. Finally, it's their turn and Charlie announces his choice.

"Sorry, I no have that one," the peddler says, with a kind of weary resignation, his stock depleted. The injustice hits Charlie hard, the notion that there can be a scarcity of what one dearly wants, and he begins to squirm.

"There's other ones, my friend," the man adds, again like he wishes darkness would come more quickly and he could make a break for it. "Sponge Bob Square Pants. Look at that red flavor." What the guy makes ferrying that contraption around must be pocket money, but the exhausted indifference, the way he keeps checking his watch grates on Brett.

"How about a Jolly Rancher?" Charlie says, already a little deflated.

"Sold-out also but we have Toasted Almond, Peanut Butter Cups, Neapolitan, Klondike Bars . . . ." The man points to their lifeless depictions on the beaten-up chassis.

For some reason, the endless loop of the tune is driving Brett crazy and makes it impossible to concentrate. It is somehow like his own mind, with its perpetual echo of mistakes.

Someone behind them mutters, "C'mon, it isn't rocket science."

"Listen, can you turn off the music for a minute," Brett pleads. "We just have to be able to hear ourselves think."

"Sir, this is how children know I'm here. Come from all around."

A flash of a memory emerges from somewhere—Brett's father getting home late, in a bad temper from having lost at a card game. By the time he gives Brett money for a cone, the hawker is long gone. His unrepaired bike not an option, Brett tries to chase the truck, but all he gets is the Pollyannaish chant receding in the distance.

"Okay, I'll give you five dollars to cut it off just for a few minutes. I feel like some of those notes are clobbering me."

"Sir, this is my calling card. How will children know Rafael is here?"

"Rafael huh, really?" Brett blurts out. "Where are the rest of your pals, Gabriel and Ariel—out saving damsels in distress?" He figures he's getting the reverse side of the angels now, the avenging aspect. And Yader keeps bubbling up in his head, how he could make things look like Brett was a one-man wrecking crew. He might have convinced the old man to let him go. The car could completely fall apart next week, then the job, and perhaps the marriage too, for the triple crown.

Rafael seems befuddled by the seraphic reference and just shrugs, palms up. The refrain must be on its fiftieth round by now, with all its pounding buoyancy, and Brett finally excavates the lyrics of the song "Do your ears hang low? Can you tie them in a bow? Do your ears hang high, do they reach up to the sky?"

Before he realizes he's even considered it, Brett hurls the football as hard as he can into the side of the vehicle, its metallic report causing the adults lounging around the tables behind them to turn his way startled, as the ball rolls end over end toward a web of chains.

"Mister, you need to relax," Rafael says, finally roused from his lethargy, although his tone seems not so much an effort to calm Brett down as to issue a warning.

"Try being me for a day and you'd realize that's impossible advice."

Charlie has become rapt with this exchange and starts looking at Brett like he's some kind of lunatic. Glancing back, he can see people whispering, shooing their kids toward the exit, and begin to reach for their devices. The line behind them disperses as if someone has spotted lightning. It's just a matter of time before the sirens will be in range, converging with their wails and circling beams.

"It's company policy. I can't turn it off," Rafael says, gathering up his stool and makeshift stand. Then, he climbs back in the cab and reaches behind the freezer for something, perhaps a pipe or tire iron kept for protection. Brett notices a piece of a log that has broken off one of the wooden towers—Tuttle's legacy breaking down like the rest of the universe. At first, he grabs it out of some instinct to ward off danger or just keep the conflict on even terms, but something in the man's look seems like a taunt, as if he can see through him to all that's gone haywire.

The last second before Brett raises the club, like Oog or Gloog, in some primordial threat, he notices Charlie's no longer there and then sees him approaching with Sara Chang. She is flushed but still forces an uneasy smile, her inherent shyness not entirely cast off.

"Mr. Hanbeck," she calls out, a little breathlessly, "Charlie's asking for a play date with Michelle next week. Are you okay?"

Brett must look absolutely deranged to Sara with that head wound in full view and the mustard splattered across his shirt like a flame. But the manner in which she nervously reaches out from so far away, as if he were drowning and she is desperate to keep him afloat, disarms him, compels him to turn back. He tosses the log over toward the bushes that rim the park, where its jagged edges will be out of the way.

"No, I'm all right," Brett announces, "just clearing a little debris."

"Charlie is so big. He must have grown a foot in six months," she says, drawing up closer, Charlie trailing beside her. Their diminished audience mostly returns to their private colloquies. Charlie seems to have forgotten about the dessert, his taste buds no match for the lure of a submarine toy he's discovered in his pocket. The vendor has gotten behind the wheel and ignited the engine. Brett thinks he should flag him down and apologize, maybe slip the guy ten bucks for all this nonsense, but he is caught in the moment, searching for a way to put everything back together again. Before he can react, the truck is gone, the last vestiges of its pitch sinking under the breeze.

"Michelle is in interpretive dance, can you believe it?" Sara says, in a more comfortable mode now, the charge in the air having been defused. Sara points in the vicinity of the bouncing house, though her daughter has already abandoned it, exploring elsewhere.

"I want to play soccer, Dad," Charlie says, seeing the checkered ball near the pile of other alternatives. Brett notices most of his son's other companions have left as dusk approaches, their parents with places to go.

"Why didn't I think of that?" Brett says, wearily grateful for any diversion just then. Sara gives him her card and tells him to call if it works out, before trotting around a set of suspended rings to locate her daughter.

"Dad, look what I found in the fountain? It looks really old or something." Brett examines the coin, with its dull painted sheen and crude markings. It must have slipped into the muddy water of the clogged drain when he went for a drink, his brain still reeling from the blow. Charlie is muttering about how it has bubbled up from some underground sea. The fact that they are a thousand miles from the coast does not seem to interfere with his logic.

"Good work, Charlie."

"And it fits right in the seat of this ship," he says, holding up another unlikely combination.

Then another image rises in Brett from when he was about Charlie's age, an amusement park with some flying craft of similar design. It's one of those rides that flings the cars around on cables in a series of revolutions, and he is too afraid to try it. His dad, cheerful that night, perhaps having had some luck with the ponies, insists it is not so perilous and they clamber aboard. He feels now their soaring as the rough motion slams them back and forth against the sides, his father's arm around him, safer than anyplace in the world.

## *Early Retirement*

Neal couldn't help but be annoyed when people reacted strangely to his early retirement. Their initial shock routinely gave way to a shallow congratulation, and after a certain interval, the bombshell would uneasily sink in. Where did he get all that loot with the economy on life support? Was his good fortune actually the result of some clandestine criminal enterprise, some off-the-books wheelings and dealings with a safe deposit box in Monaco? He could almost read these inner queries like a teleprompter radiating across the faint lines of their faces. He knew that this questioning was not malice so much as mere curiosity, of the kind any detective novel worth reading would produce. And Neal looked younger than he was, which may have added to the sense that something was awry.

Everywhere he went, he seemed to overhear a remark reinforcing the fact that he'd become an outcast, which in ancient societies was tantamount to a death sentence. The mood of the country was sour, even belligerent. The national debt was in such bad shape that scapegoats and pariahs were necessary. In Barrymore's, a nearby watering hole where he and Rita often went for Factoid Night, Neal eavesdropped on a woman he recognized as one of the regulars. She had a small tattoo depicting a sunrise at the base of her shoulder and was intermittently shrill in her certainty that the questions were rigged.

During a break, as she sat with what must have been a gang of acquaintances, she launched into a harangue, using that voice which was designed to carry. "These people with their cushy pensions, their security blankets financed by you know who. Everybody knows we can't afford that nonsense anymore. It's welfare plain and simple." The woman, who wore enough costume jewelry to be in a Mardi Gras parade, glanced at Neal from time to time, as if her remarks were aimed in his general direction.

True, he was getting a tiny allowance for grimly manning a desk at the Department of Labor since the mid-eighties, but that job represented only a part of his modest wealth. Never mind that he'd never so much as collected unemployment, that he'd called in sick only five times since Reagan was president, and that some mornings his bones seemed as brittle as the tusks of a Woolly Mammoth.

"In the old days, those folks would have fallen by the wayside," the soprano rambled on, "and the species would have been better for it."

Neal was tempted to respond, but he already felt exposed with Rita unable to come that evening. Further complicating matters, the other two friends who usually helped form a team had begged off with paper-thin excuses. So, he retreated to the banter of three perfect strangers at his table. They were pleasant enough but clearly unimpressed with his sole contribution thus far, that the Blue Whale was the world's largest mammal, which was admittedly something an average third grader knew.

A couple of scotches later, just as Neal's guess that Euripides had written *Antigone* proved incorrect, he overheard another piece of the lady's rambling invective. "Nobody ever gave me a dime," she blurted; "and if they did, I'd throw it back and say, no thanks."

He knew better than to approach her in a threatening manner but begged off the rest of the game and upon his exit, leaned over. "The envy is running pretty thick in here," he said, above the sounds of clinking glasses and chairs scraping across the oak floor. "Work yourself into a premature grave if money is that important to you. Maybe you'll fulfill some burning desire to see the Colliseum and the Arc de Triumph, if you know what those are. If not, look them up. They might come in handy for the bonus round."

After Neal reluctantly mentioned his new status to Dr. Archibald, the physician who had treated him for twenty years, the usual pre-exam chit-chat seemed to vanish. Gone was the genial kidding about golf handicaps and bridge tournaments. Their interaction became strictly clinical, and the way he tested Neal's structural soundness with the rubber hammer, like he was a two-by-four at a construction site, made him feel manhandled.

He figured the reaction to his surplus fell in the same category as someone winning a lottery, though there were slightly different dynamics. In that case, people knew where the money came from—the happenstance of a random number. But this kind of luck was entirely different, with the context shrouded in personal history. It was always just too awkward to explain that he had no children and tended to live like a monk, perhaps a recessive trait from his grandfather who had gone bust in the Depression and his mother's tales of the experience, which verged on opera. Neal had salted away every dollar he could, eschewing the expensive restaurants, luxury SUV's and oversized mortgages of his contemporaries. Yet the real reason he'd been able to quit was a big bet on a security—Shotwell Corporation—which made high-tech hand dryers and faucets that were activated by a force field.

It was remarkable that he'd even bought the stock in the first place. When he initially considered dipping his toe in the market, he had a vivid dream. His grandfather appeared out of nowhere washing his hands. He was smiling, and, when he pointed to the faucet, instead of water coming out, it gushed with thousand dollar bills. The reverie could have meant anything, but Neal had an irrational conviction that it represented a tip communicated from the afterlife by his hard-luck ancestors, bent on evening the score. Since the purchase, Shotwell had rocketed up eight hundred and sixty-seven percent and become a sensation. Every time the equity announced some ridiculous dividend, he placed a fresh bouquet of flowers at the family plot. Yet, despite the turn of events, Neal did not conduct himself with the conspicuous opulence of a Powerball winner, but simply as a man who had given up the chase.

To be fair, there were a few who seemed to accept his modest success at face value, who did not seek out alternative scenarios, even if they were the exceptions. One notably authentic response had come from a clerk who bagged items at Fisher's, the local grocery. Bernard was voluble, no doubt wanting to divert himself from the deadly slog of wedging cereal boxes and pork chops into a sack all day.

"Way to go," he said enthusiastically. "You did it right, man. Not blowing every nickel as soon as it fell in your hand."

Neal was embarrassed he'd let news of his retirement slip in the first place, but Bernard had peppered him with questions he couldn't easily dodge. For a second, he recalled the surge of liberation he'd felt that first morning when he rolled over in bed and imagined his former self racing to the subway. There would be no more grappling with the insoluble riddles which awaited him at the office, the slew of claims piling up like a foggy accident on the turnpike. For a couple months, he experienced a kind of bliss he had not felt since his schooldays, when the final bell rang and a leisurely summer beckoned.

"Just blind luck," Neal said, not really believing that.

"Oh no," Bernard said, shaking his head wildly as he placed the bulging paper bag in the cart. "You beat the game. I'm going to do like that. I intend to quit while I'm still alive."

After a couple weeks of utter sloth, sifting through every word in his backlog of *Barron's* and *Vanity Fair,* Neal became restless. At first, he thought he might want to write a biography of some figure who'd been overlooked by history, but the more he considered the rigors involved, the more it seemed like a mountain he didn't really want to climb. Vacations with Rita to Ireland and Greece lay in some vague planning stage. Yet upon seeing a movie involving a plane crash, they'd both gotten too rattled even to peruse the brochures.

With two grown sons from a previous marriage, Rita was content to have the kind of monogamous, non-contractual relationship that felt stable without the sense that it was sealed in eternity. She lived with Neal and had been designated his heir, but was often gone. She liked the rhythms of work and would have been lost without her coffee klatch, which skewered the bosses in a festive way. She was content with their modest bungalow, and when their financial advisor gave the go-ahead, hadn't insisted he remain a captive of his labyrinthine bureaucracy. Golf increasingly bored Neal with its interminable waiting, and he had no interest in lounging around cafes making small talk with strangers. So he embarked on a series of trips to museums, aquariums, zoos, and other points of interest, most of which he'd ignored for decades.

Of these, the most intriguing was the Universe Institute. Neal didn't know a great deal about astronomy, but there was something about the grandness of its subject that offered relief from the secrets and pettiness of his own planet. On his second visit, after emerging from a spectacular sky show that illustrated the vastness of the stars, he volunteered to become a part-time docent. He took a four-hour orientation, during which he managed a superficial understanding of the principle terms and concepts.

For all of October, he gladly sacrificed his Thursday mornings to wide-eyed tourists and children who clamored and flitted about the exhibits like a flock of seagulls. Though Neal was assigned to the least sexy room they had—an illustration of the solar system that lacked the interactive bells and whistles of the other wings—no one asked him why he was no longer sitting zombie-like in a cubicle. It all went fine until a substitute boss showed up one day, the polar opposite of the affable matron he'd replaced. Mr. Horax had a Greek accent and the mien of a tenured professor.

"What brings you to us? Are you in the telescope society?" Horax inquired, with a hint of condescension. He looked like one of those people who are certain of the abject ignorance of the general populace. "We get a few of those."

It occurred to Neal that the only time he had ever peered through one of the instruments was when his college roommate set up a perch to ogle coeds across the quad. "No, I just had some time on my hands," he stammered.

"Prison release?" Mr. Horax asked, his eyes twinkling with a sardonic edge. "Just kidding. It's none of my business. Listen, we've got a monster field trip scheduled. Do you mind subbing in the Deep Space Room today?"

Neal was glad for the chance to man that section, which had a fantastic diorama on dark matter and was less claustrophobic. School kids had already begun to stream in like the lobby was a combat perimeter being overrun. Before he knew it, a troop from Rutledge Academy accosted him where he stood near a screen full of whirling galaxies. Still unsettled by Horax's insinuations, surrounded by loud scientific homilies and a platform of revolving discs, he tried to recall all the material he'd crammed in from the volunteer booklet. Neal had used precious little of it at his usual display, which, after all, had only a few celestial objects to memorize.

"Sir, what can you tell us about this," said their exhausted teacher, Ms. Balsam, a woman in her thirties who kept count of her wards by pointing at each of them like a lifeguard.

"Okay, well that's the Lobster Nebula. It's just about in the middle of Alpha Centauri." That was what came back to him when he'd begun the answer, but by the end, the information seemed to whiz back and forth like asteroids in the Kuiper Belt. Neal felt a bead of sweat on his forehead as he wondered if his response could withstand close inspection. Ms. Balsam initially seemed preoccupied with her herding instincts, but as soon as he finished, she blinked a number of times and a patch of redness began migrating at the base of her neck.

"I'm sorry but that just can't be right. We just studied this last week."

"Perhaps I could get one of our roaming scholars. I'm a bit new." There was an agonizing moment when he thought she might charge off and summon the director, but for some reason she relented.

"Never mind, what about that over there?" Ms. Balsam gestured toward a chart that supposedly followed time back to the Big Bang. "Can you enlighten us?"

Neal was buoyed that this was a question he could handle and, with at least a few of the huddled students intent on his reply, he was determined to knock it out of the park. "Sure, it shows how the universe began twelve million years ago."

"Really?" the indignant schoolmarm snapped "This isn't supposed to be some science-fiction trip. From what I've heard so far, I don't think you could locate the moon on a clear night."

Neal frantically tried to ferret out the source of his mistake, but it was no good and as it turned out, she wasn't the type to let any fraud remain unexposed. When he was let go, on the way out, he deliberately misinformed an elderly gentleman, who looked like he was plastered and had wandered in to avoid a charge of vagrancy. Neal told him that the sun could implode and become a useless white dwarf at any moment. "You better warn the grandkids," he said in a conspiratorial whisper. "It won't emit any more light than a lava lamp."

Not long after, there was a graduation party for Neal's niece. He might have skipped it and sent a card, but Chloe was that rare member of the next generation who occasionally acknowledged his existence. Neal was accustomed to being cast at the bottom of the totem pole, to having his occasional remarks ignored and interrupted, and his infrequent opinions being dismissed as soon as he left the room. Being childless, he was already regarded as a dead end, a lifeless branch in the Chappell lineage.

His siblings were scattered all over the suburbs as if they had parachuted at various stages, and Neal had not yet announced his retirement to them. He knew they were bound to be suspicious and caught off guard. Without telling Rita, he had amassed a list of additional charges that might silently be leveled against him, pieced together from a number of evasive remarks. Had he been a tax dodger all these years, leaving the rest of them to pay for several wars, the crushing medical costs of the elderly, and a national debt, which if placed in a big pile would stretch to Saturn? Was he some unsavory gigolo who was sponging off a smitten and impossibly gullible divorcee? Or, perhaps his favorite theory: he had gone off his rocker, deluded himself that he had enough to last all the way to the grave, having no clue about the intricacies of finance, such that he would soon find himself high and dry.

The brother he most worried about was Brent, five years his senior, a prosperous home remodeler, former star of his university's tennis team, and president of the local Kiwanis club. He had a stable of friends who would fall on a grenade for him, a sprawling house, as well as an abiding love of brandy and elaborate gags. The latter was in the tradition of revered Uncle Conrad, whose anecdotes were the stuff of off-color legend and whose pranks bordered on cruelty. He had instigated so many wild goose chases that Neal's aunts seemed to adopt a permanent air of disbelief. However, the unwritten code they had all inherited was that kidding, even rough kidding, was to be tolerated for the sake of some temporary reprieve from the grim facts of life. The problem was that some of these ruses carried things too far.

The month before Neal quit, Brent called him at the office using one of his myriad accents, Indian this time, full of odd cadences and pitches in the middle of words. He knew that Neal parked in a questionable place—a kind of no man's land—to avoid the ridiculous fees charged at the downtown lots. Brent said he was from Barbarossa Towing, that Neal had violated ordinance 369F, and that his vehicle had been conveyed to a distant receiving yard, via hoist and a set of chains. He told Neal with his almost incomprehensible pronunciations that if he didn't pay the exorbitant fine and retrieve the car within forty-eight hours, it would be crushed and sold as scrap.

Brent hurriedly gave an address that was miles to the east in a district near the expressway. Neal had a meeting in two minutes, so he tried to mute his dismay and assured the would-be dispatcher he would be there in time. Brent let him brood about this ordeal for hours, consider the damage his shocks had suffered jouncing over countless potholes at a forty-five degree angle, dragged like a prisoner. It wasn't until he was just about to leave that Neal received another call. As he sifted through his sales receipts, Brent laughed heartily at the other end of the line, saying "Do you know how many Bollywood movies I had to watch to get the dialect right?"

Neal's retirement wasn't aimed at the rest of the family like a missile in some endless game of one-upmanship, but unfortunately that's how Brent took it when his younger brother mumbled the news. The announcement was met with the kind of hush he had so seldom been afforded, yet it wasn't the stunned celebratory intake of breath that accompanied some major milestone. It was more like he had just declared a stunning and unforeseeable checkmate.

"You're putting me on." Brent's eyes seemed to be searching for some sign this was one of Neal's misfired jokes.

"No, I have the cheap statue with a maudlin engraving to prove it."

"Well, good for you," Brent said, with a frightening intensity. He scanned the kitchen, which was like one of his showrooms, with a faux marble island, shaped like the deck of an aircraft carrier, in the middle, but none of this helped him absorb the blow. His gaze landed on the cabinet where his best brandies were stored, the Remi Martin, Courvoisier, and Alambic, as if he wanted to take a swig directly from the bottle, though it was barely two o'clock. "How long were you at the department?"

"Nearly three decades, with a bit more credited for not bolting sooner."

Despite Brent's meteoric rise, he still had three more college diplomas to underwrite, such that he would probably be in harness until he was seventy.

"How'd you pull it off?" Brent asked, barely keeping the exasperation out of his voice.

"Shotwell Industries. Nine thousand shares." Rita was off taking pictures of Chloe cutting the cake in her cap and gown, so that she was not there to shield him. Talking about money was always in bad taste, and Neal had never even mentioned his investments. Yet he felt maneuvered into a corner and calculated that absolute frankness was the best way to deflect a counterattack.

"But haven't they been getting whacked lately?" Brent followed the markets religiously but often complained of their inscrutable swings.

"Don't worry. All the bases are covered." In another fortuitous development, Neal had jumped out just as the corporation, burdened now with so much media scrutiny, began to collapse under its own weight.

"Hey, everybody," Brent shouted toward the porch, no longer able to contain himself. "Neal's suddenly a guzzillionaire. He's flown the coop."

Noise from a score of exchanges reverberated across the yard, as Brent guided him into the center of a legion of relatives. The lawn was strewn with the equipment of a half dozen sports. There was a small inflatable pool, a hockey net, spikes for horseshoes, a trampoline, an archery target, and a catcher's glove.

"Aren't you a mysterious fellow," his sister Marge chided him, as several others including Rita, gathered around in a scrum.

"It's always the quiet ones," her husband Todd said, with a nudge to Neal's ribs. He could almost see Todd scrolling through his history. Hadn't he been almost broke years ago? Hadn't he been seen shopping in Goodwill thrift stores well into his 30's? Didn't he drive a decrepit Dodge Valero until it had been condemned as a public hazard?

"Chloe is just beautiful," Rita interjected, in a desperate attempt to change the flow of conversation. "How did she grow up so fast?" The Chapells had accepted Rita, embracing her emigration from Belgrade, gradually supplanting him in their subtle loyalties. It was as if Neal and Rita's bloodlines had somehow been switched. That few of them could have located her home country on a map seemed to muddy the situation even further. They continued to circle around Neal like an aboriginal hunting party, cutting off every avenue of escape. Brent had adopted a wide stance, as if he were preparing for a wrestling match, and had partially crushed his can of Sprite.

"C'mon Neal, tell us the real story," Brent said, a malevolent gleam in his eye. "You're among friends." Neal couldn't blame Brent for letting off some steam, but his providence was a touchy subject, and Neal wasn't in the mood. He'd already divulged too much and anything more would just seem like gloating.

"What do you want—twenty years of tax records?" he shot back, rising to the bait. "There's nothing in the Cayman's, I assure you. I did it fair and square."

"Me thinks he doth protest too much," Brent bellowed, to a round of giggles Rita pretended to blend in with. "I have to hand it to you though, getting that sweet government gig, latching onto the gravy train, even as we sink like the Roman Empire."

Rita must have seen that Neal was about to blow like Vesuvius because she began furiously fanning herself. The way she was flapping her wrists resembled some pitiful attempt to fly. "Ah, this heat," she emoted, "I'm getting a little faint."

The diversion was enough to forestall the kind of vile rejoinder which Neal was capable of, one that would have sent a tremor through the entire neighborhood. Marge rushed Rita into the shade, brought her several cups of water and in five minutes, after a gang of Chloe's cohorts arrived, Rita spirited Neal away.

On the ride home, Neal resisted the urge to call Rita a turncoat for not coming to his defense. Despite that considerable self restraint, someone must have put a bug in her ear because she suddenly seemed intent on launching him into some grand project, "to keep him out of trouble."

"They're always talking about the president's legacy. Why not do something to secure yours?" she advised, as he cursed speeders on the interstate.

"What if I were to ghost write a book called *A History of Indolence*?" he offered.

Neal had taken up smoking again, just a few Parliaments a week after having kicked the habit in college, and this relapse didn't help matters. There was also some strange coolness in Rita he could not recall encountering before. Since the Universe Institute debacle, Neal felt more and more like a loose cannon, failing to engage in any meaningful activity beyond simple chores. Most of the people he knew were still juggling a dozen different agendas, making him feel like a worthless bystander. Even if he wanted to devote himself to unbridled repose, he lacked a cadre of unfettered companions with whom to share it.

The next weekend there was another party, this one a fundraiser that was certain to attract an assortment of people from the community who had not yet gotten wind of his story. Rita was eager to go because a few of her closest friends would be there, and she loved the idea that she could dance and sing and appease her conscience with a donation all at once.

After she dressed and Neal pretended to do the same, he grabbed a bottle of Johnny Walker and barricaded himself in their bedroom. To thwart any entrance, he shoved the bureau of drawers, solid as a sarcophagus, half way across the room. There was a lock on the door, but it was flimsy and he didn't want to take any chances.

"What are you doing in there?" she berated him.

"I'm scouring the real estate sites for a cave. That's what I want. A cave with internet. A cave where there's a tavern within an hour's camel ride."

"Neal, don't be ridiculous. We're going to be late." Her tone of pique was not diluted by the plaster walls.

"I can't stand it anymore, the way people treat you like you're a munitions dealer. Like you just sold the H-bomb to Al Qaida."

Looking absently out the window, he noted that some kids had stolen one of the magnetic letters from the sign in front of the Episcopal Church across the parkway because its New Testament quotation read "Blessed are the pacemakers." The message that changed every week sometimes managed to give him a lift and even that small measure of spiritual solace seemed to have been withdrawn. By this point, the veneers had peeled away, so that all Neal's previous endeavors were being dismantled and cast in an insidious light. His roommate from Rutgers, who had always believed him without reservation, sent him an email that read: "So sorry to find out you were drawn into that pyramid scheme. I have every confidence you'll be fully exonerated . . . ."

There were times when he really didn't give a damn what people thought because they were almost always getting it wrong. They saw a fraction of how it was and would extrapolate the rest with a thousand wildly mistaken inferences. Neal tried to cheer himself with the fact that his daily reprieve from the frenetic streets of downtown, the crammed elevators and relentless competition was not, as often happened, due to some catastrophic news. He had not actually been hit by a bus, become the victim of a tornado, or some mortifying viral episode. Yet, he'd begun to wonder if tragedy might have been preferable, since at least that would have injected a sympathetic element.

"You can't hide the rest of your life like some kind of crackpot," Rita pleaded. "I need camaraderie and laughter. A few good stories once in a while."

"Social engagement is overrated. With Peapod and a satellite dish, you don't have to go out for months."

She grabbed her keys and charged for the door, but not before he shouted, "Tell them I've contracted Ebola and have been placed in quarantine, but not to worry."

In retrospect, that was the moment when Neal hit bottom, when he knew that he needed some radical new plan to redirect his life, like a swollen river seizing a new tributary. He could beg for his old job back, but he had burned numerous bridges, and besides, his Facebook page was full of pictures of his former colleagues flourishing in the wake of his departure.

Neal considered several kinds of desperate getaways but each had a critical drawback. He could move to Bombay or Camaroon or Guatemala to work in a leper colony, though the heat would kill him before the germs ever had a chance. He could simply slink off to Kansas City in the middle of the night, despite the fact everyone's suspicion of guilt would be confirmed, and he would be branded a mobster. It even occurred to him that he could fake his own death, a skiing accident perhaps, or a skydiving mishap over a remote area. Yet, these disasters would require a degree of guile he didn't possess, and Rita would never go along with such preposterous stunts.

That night he had another indelible dream, this time about Bernard, who had disappeared from Fisher's some months before. He wore a tuxedo and rode in the back of a glistening limousine, with a wide screen TV and a wet bar. It was clear he was on his third or fourth martini despite the sunshine outside, and he sat grimly watching one of those talk shows where there is a challenge of paternity, as the whole studio awaits the salacious result. Neal wanted to call out to Bernard, to wish him well, but the scene cut to the chauffer who was sealed off from his passenger. In contrast, the driver was beaming, though whether the source of his happiness issued from the memory of a child romping in the park or the simple beauty of shadows filtering through the elms, was impossible to know.

Neal could never quite trace the origin of the ploy he chose to rectify the situation, yet he was sure Bernard had somehow rescued him again. He reasoned that if people began to hate him for striking it rich, they would love him doubly were he to experience a great reversal. Shotwell happened to be in its final death throes, and the business channels were broadcasting those nonstop, as enthralled as spectators watching someone on the ledge of a skyscraper. Well aware that word of his antics would spread like an epidemic, Neal staged a kind of breakdown in Barrymore's, ranting at his iPhone as the headline about the company's liquidation was highlighted under the sinister company logo.

He remained out of sight for a while and then began working a few hours a week at Fisher's, dressing more shabbily than ever, mimicking the sort of battered, desolate look of those who have made some catastrophic error. He resumed his old habits of frugality with a vengeance. It wasn't difficult to return to that former asceticism once he made the transition, and he felt invigorated for the first time in ages.

Neal was in charge of gathering up the carts and ushering them back into the store. This assignment gave him an opportunity to stretch his legs and grab a smoke near the bays where they unloaded the trailers. He was fascinated to see the operation from that vantage, the carcasses and fruit and produce hauled and unloaded. In the beginning, it was like being behind the curtain at a Broadway show.

During his shift at the end of the counter, he was determined not to act like the post was some sentenced community service. He followed Bernard's example, remaining steadfastly cheerful, even in the midst of customers who ran the entire gamut of boredom and impatience. Neal knew he was performing a vital function in society, that every person who entered his checkout aisle was someone who could benefit from some brief, pleasant exchange. It made everything easier that he still had his 1.4 million in bonds stashed away, though no one else besides Rita knew. She would sometimes come into his line, pretend he was a stranger, put on the airs of a finicky shopper and ask him to rearrange the purchases in the bags. Once she adlibbed, "Didn't I always see you at Granville Station-waiting for the 7:42?"

"Yes, I had a little setback," he improvised. "But I like being around food. Believe me, things could be a lot worse." The skits only got more enjoyable when they bought a cabin cruiser, christened *The Windfall*, which was docked a few towns north.

Neal was surprised at how kind many people were when he signaled his acceptance of the whims of fate with a steady, welcoming eye contact. His neighbors were especially cordial, not for a second betraying their ridicule or pity. As predicted, word had traveled at the speed of light about his supposed ruin. Neal suspected it was a regular topic at parties he had once been invited to and would soon be again. His family must have had a field day with their "I told you so's," but kept those among themselves, and rallied in support whenever the circumstances required.

Dr. Archibald happened in one evening for some avocados. He couldn't have been nicer, patting Neal on the back as he handed over the packages, and even asking his patient's advice on how to cure a wicked hook. The tattooed woman from the trivia contest shot him a glare of warning when she first came in, but offered a warm smile when he made sure her eggs and cauliflower didn't get crushed. A strange serenity had come over him, the calm he had always imagined would surface when the burdens of commerce were laid down. It must have seemed odd Neal was so content to be a figure of stupendous folly, but given that the truth was otherwise, he basked in the part, having been restored to old his tribe.

## *Trouble with The Magi*

In June, when golf balls were still occasionally flying into my backyard and being tallied as a kind of harvest, my wife Laney's Great Aunt Marian died. She was very old and, in contemplation of the end, had somehow managed the demeanor of someone embarking on a cruise. As part of the business of will and probate, we were forced to sort the things in her house to see what was worth keeping. I was up in the attic where the heat was as thick and palpable as fog. There was the usual clutter of ancient suitcases and obsolete appliances, with no apparent antique value, all for the most part a repository of junk.

But I also came upon some interesting items, which had belonged to Laney's great grandfather, most notably a journal and a staff. The latter was comprised of smooth dark wood that curled at the top like a helix, which Everett had used to traverse the uneven local countryside. We returned home, put the staff up on the recreation room wall and took turns reading the notebooks. This chronicle consumed me for weeks, especially as I had only the vaguest knowledge of the man. There were only a couple of faded, extant pictures of him, a shock of wild gray hair and eyes that smoldered like hot coals. Like many ancestors beyond our reach, he seemed a figure obscured by distance, a man hidden inside a mask.

This opening to the past seemed to have an effect on Laney. She tended to be fascinated by the eccentric, but the practical side of her nature had always confined this interest to an occasional tabloid in a checkout line. Besides the diary, Marian had stockpiled books on the paranormal, some even going back to Everett's day, and Laney read them like an addict. Now, it was as if some dormant proclivity in her genes had been set loose. She began frequenting health-food stores and attending seminars on herbal remedies. Laney had always been frugal in the purchase of clothes, but now ran up huge bills at "Earthrise" with essences, balms, and antidotes to every imagined ailment. I cringed every time I drove by the storefront, with its primeval globe, Yin/Yang symbol, and Celtic Runes on atavistic display.

Part of the problem may have been that she wanted another baby, but we were having trouble conceiving one. In keeping with her natural bent, she didn't want to try anything scientific but some superstitious variations, which frankly I did not altogether object to, were employed. I will not reveal them here, except to say that they involved incense, different rooms of the house, some alchemical mumbo jumbo, and in one memorable instance, a wand.

"You know my line is fertile, Brock. Everett may have been a philanderer, but he had fourteen children," Laney said one evening, as she flipped through a magazine filled with placid infants. "Fourteen. That we know of . . . ." Her features darkened the way the way they did when someone in a sports car cut her off on the turnpike.

"Don't worry sweetheart. We're just in a little slump," I said, distracted by some ridiculous commercial.

"Oh, I guess that explains everything," she said, staring vacantly out toward the swings in the backyard.

"Even Willie Mays, one of the greatest hitters of all time, once went 0 for 22." I guess it wasn't the most soothing thing to say as she abruptly bolted upstairs.

Later that Fall, which was cool and prismatic, she somehow heard about a series of Friday night "salons" in a "comfortable Jupiterian space." The poster promised discussions of mandalas, shamanic rituals, and karmic stone trances. I knew that a psychologist in the area, Mitch Prevane, sometimes went to these outings and knowledge of his participation irked me to no end. He specialized in phobias, more than just the ones you hear about: fear of mathematics, fear of subways, fear of hail. His wife was the remote type, and there were rumors that he tended to stray.

I suppose I had never quite recovered from my one encounter with him a few years back when Laney and I hit a rough patch. Though the issue was quickly solved, despite rather than because of Prevane, the episode left an indelible mark. The way it was set up, we were to see him separately the first time and then jointly later on. Prevane had strange ideas about icons and totems, which were cast about his office like hexes. I could not have been more uncomfortable than if I had attended a heinous voodoo ceremony. Laney had the initial sessions and then it was my turn. You could tell that Mitch was adept at putting people at ease, and, for a while, he made a point to chat like someone at a cocktail party. But at some prearranged moment, he subtly honed in on the supposed defects of my private life.

"What's this about a half hour when no one is permitted to speak to you? Laney mentioned something about that rule in passing." He was referring to my habit of heading to a section of the basement set up with an old sofa, a temperamental lamp, and a second-hand stereo for a short while after I got home. It was there I stashed my archaic tape collection and a few astronomy journals. Some of the tapes were nothing but sounds: nightingales in a castle courtyard, waves beating against a shoreline, the haunting cry of loons across a lake somewhere. It was just a means of transition from one set of conundrums to another.

"Well, it's just a time to decompress, a brief respite, a few minutes to myself," I said.

"Is it a kind of meditation?"

"No, I don't go in for that sort of thing."

"The Chinese have been doing it for thousands of years."

"Good for them."

"What do you do down there exactly?" Mitch sat in a gargantuan leather chair from which he bestowed his rarified observations. Though he was pleasant enough, there was something I disliked about his chiseled jaw and the way his eyes seemed to drift and then stare right through me.

"I just read, listen to headphones . . . . Look, I do the dishes nearly every night. I play with my kids to the point of exhaustion. I shovel the snow, mow the grass. Laundry has never been a terrible chore. I bring a book, and the sight of clothes tumbling round and round is strangely soothing."

"Do you sometimes dream of other women in a provocative way?" The question was so brazen, so calculated and out of context, I was seized by an urge to leap out of the recliner and knock him senseless, but such mayhem would just have handed him a load of ammunition. All I could bring myself to say was "plenty" before storming out.

Laney stopped going too, but found other evening diversions, which were forcing me to take up the lion's share of domestic maintenance. Gone was my brief interval of nightly solitude pouring over supernovas and gamma ray bursts. The children seemed to have grown more and more rebellious under my watch, and the price of getting them into bed at a reasonable hour had become exorbitant. The situation deteriorated further when I bought a snowmobile in November when the sales were at their highest pitch. The idea of barreling through a shoot of trees and feeling the landscape beneath me seemed to lift my spirits, but Laney seemed to view the purchase as some breach of contract.

The night after the delivery truck backed up to the garage with the sleek machine, she announced she was planning to attend a lunar festival for the weekend. I thought we had agreed to take the kids to the aquarium, and some intemperate remarks were exchanged. In the back of my mind, a suspicion formed that she was at least flirting with Prevane. The soft, sheltering fall had given way to the denuded clarification of winter. That's the way I thought of it; not the plunge of temperature so much as the disappearance of wildlife and the feeling of an abandoned resort. The vacant nests were suddenly visible, as if caught in the intricate web of branches like wayward kites. Still, the scent of burning leaves was among my favorites, together with woodsmoke, coriander and lilac, all of which led me back to some indistinct sense of origin.

Not long afterwards, Laney read in the church bulletin that Father Gilroy was planning to stage a nativity skit for midnight mass, and she wanted to be in it. The parents were going to perform for a change because the last version had turned into a debacle of forgotten lines, contagious hysterics, and hurled straw. I knew it might mean a few more "Hungry Man" TV dinners and a missed card game or two, but it seemed a preferable alternative to the other archaic nonsense. Laney had done a little acting in high school, and I thought this reprise might divert her from the disappointment of not getting pregnant on schedule. She had been used to a certain time table, as if a baby were something you just ordered over the phone.

One day she came home a little breathless and spoke so rapidly, for a minute I felt I needed an interpreter. The upshot was she had won the part of the blessed virgin. She added that there was an opening for the village innkeeper who refuses lodging for the holy couple. At first, I was adamant about staying out of the production. Nevertheless, the chance to play the heavy, to vent any latent reserves of meanness must have appealed to me, so I agreed to do it. My acquiescence was not a minute old before Laney announced that Prevane was to be one of the wise men. It again occurred to me that his path seemed to be crossing with Laney's more often than might be explained by serendipity. In fact, I remembered how enamored she had been with the counseling and became convinced she was falling in love with him.

On most days, the sound of Laney's voice was such a tonic that the absence of it could exert a pressure like a blow to the solar plexus. The gentleness in her eyes, the angle of her sweeping hair can elicit such a buoyance that I feel light as a cork. But as the performance drew nearer, she seemed to become more and more immersed in her role. Laney was sleeping so far over on the other side of the bed, it was like she was in another area code. She was having dreams where angels appeared, but instead of imparting some grave and astounding message, they announced what would happen next in her favorite soap opera, *Stonewell's Creek*.

The Yuletide sketch was to be staged in the historic barn, which was the sole surviving vestige from the onslaught of our development. Its structure was left standing by the real estate moguls despite their zeal to level everything else—as a draw for harried urbanites, a symbol of the bucolic pace of days gone by.

The barn had a door you could drive a semi through, a loft, and motes of light sifting through the cracks. The fading paint had turned to an umber hue, which only enhanced its charm. It was weathered, fragile as plywood, as if it were made out of a mountain of matchsticks assembled by some obsessive hermit. Voting booths were set up there for primaries and elections and Mrs. Geiger, one of the original settlers, appropriated a section for a periodic community rummage sale. I always enjoyed seeing the rafters, the irregular angles of the roof, idiosyncratic as a shoreline.

At one of the early rehearsals, when Laney and Prevane were huddling with the director over the final scene, Jim Nederland, who was to portray one of the shepherds, came over to complain that we were being treated like extras. Jim was an usher at the church, and it seemed odd to see him not holding a basket of checks and crumpled bills.

"You know you're pretty far down the program when you don't even get a name. I'm just #2," Jim said, in his deadpan manner, as he scanned the room.

"Hey, you look fine though," I said, noting his sack-like outfit. "Not like Balthazar over there." I motioned toward Prevane, who was waving a cigarette around, despite the fact that the place could go up like kindling. Here was a man who could somehow solve other people's complex problems yet couldn't help but ruin his own lungs.

"Yeah, a bit much."

In his spangled robes, Prevane looked like a corrupt judge. He was the only one with a crown, the jagged edges resembling shark teeth one of his kids made in art class. He didn't seem to hover about Laney, perhaps by pre-arrangement to avoid suspicion but leaned over to her a couple times to make some private remark. I was under instructions not to talk to her because she thought this would wreck her concentration and she would forget the lines. My costume at that point merely consisted of a leather vest with tassels and some hat from the sixties, which was half way between a fez and a bellboy cap.

Laney had the idea to use the staff in the play. "The more authenticity the better," she said, as she rifled through a box of old scarves. I had begun to notice how strange I felt holding it, as if I had seen years rush past and was suddenly wizened. But then, the next minute, there was the reverse effect, and I seemed filled with all the vigor and ebullience of youth. Even though the staff should really go to one of the shepherds, Laney had aready lent it to Prevane, whereupon he swaggered around with it like an emperor.

"Mitch, try to be careful with that. It's an heirloom," I said, trying to soften the degree of my irritation, yet still get the point across.

"Of course. It's a beauty. I could have used this on the 17th hole last year." He did a half swing almost jabbing Melchior in the ribs.

Prevane walked over to the guy playing Joseph and started goading him to take a tougher stand on the lodging issue, but the man, who looked more like a wrestler than a Bible figure, sensibly resisted. With Prevane filling the stage with an obtuse majesty, I had chosen to understate my role, while still playing the character as a beleaguered victim of circumstance. Father Gilroy was firm that we shouldn't take too many liberties with the language, even though scripture was laconic on the subject. Still, even by the third run through, I couldn't help myself and offered to take Mary and Joseph's bags out to the stable.

As it happened, the following night, Laney was off to another seminar with hardly a word, and I met Renna Hilliard at an impromptu party at the Rosavitos. Nederland's daughter was able to come over and watch the kids for a while, so I went. To my amazement, Renna was interested in astronomy, a topic that had fascinated me since high school, but which had languished in the face of Laney's disdain for the scientific.

"Did you know that during the summer, we're facing toward the center of the Milky Way and in the winter, toward the edge?" Renna asked.

"Yes, not many people know that."

"That's why the sky is clearer now. Not so many suns to haze things up."

There is no more potent aphrodisiac than the intersection of a rare interest. I could have hurled her onto the couch right there in our neighbor's family room. Our conversation covered quasars, nebula, black holes, red giants, and other arcane subjects most people would find the most implausible excuse to avoid. Renna had a slight, almost angular build and was not as pretty as Laney, but the flirtatious tilt of her head, the novelty of her coyness and hint of unfamiliar perfume made something give way. She had what all forbidden lovers possess—an otherness, the lure of a separate life, the delight of recovered possibility. By the end of the evening, Renna was leaning into my shoulder with an almost complete absence of reserve, and I knew we would see each other again.

There was a motel about ten miles outside of Windhaven called the Starlight. It was pressed up against Mirror Lake, and the rooms were given names of the constellations; Orion, Perseus, Andromeda, Gemini, Cassiopeia. Given my interest in the heavens, the motel would have been my choice for a tryst even if it had been condemned, but it was reasonably clean and quiet. The neon sign in front had triple alternating marquee lights for the words "pool," "vacancy" and "WiFi," but the outer ones framing the inner had some bad bulbs, so the omissions made it like a crossword puzzle. There was a swinging bench and a raised lantern on a small terraced lawn overlooking a meager beach. Sounds carried across on the lake: propeller planes, fish flipping to the surface, a train's fading rush. Just being in the exotic hideaway put us in the playful mode of affairs on the upswing, of surrendering to something taboo. Renna would tease me, saying, "Darling, since you're an adjuster, would you adjust this?" turning to reveal the clasp of a bra or unfastened zipper of her skirt.

The afternoon of our final rendezvous, when our luck ran out, there was some convention for people who were exceedingly fond of certain old TV shows like *Mash* and *Hawaii Five-0*, and simply could not accept their cancellation from the airwaves. I thought I had an agreement with the manager for a floating reservation every Thursday afternoon, but he said that the rerun folks insisted on taking every room, and he couldn't argue with that kind of business.

Maybe I was doubly incensed by my upcoming role as innkeeper whose character had been transformed into a benign and avuncular man who did the best he possibly could with a difficult situation. By contrast, this reprobate with gaudy slacks and an array of nervous tics seemed a traitor to his profession.

"I'm sorry but we're not the only place in the country with a bed for rent," he said. Armed with my certain knowledge that the situation could be handled with greater finesse, I took a swing at him, but he was more agile than he appeared, and I merely stumbled against the counter. "That's going to cost you," he said evenly, as if this were a regular response, and we left.

My furtive calls went unanswered the following week. Sometimes, there is nothing more poignant than a phone that just keeps ringing and you think it's going to be picked up on the next one and then the next. Renna had even unplugged the answering machine, and it was almost anticlimactic when I got a note the day before Christmas Eve at the office. Clearly, she didn't want to dwell on something so lamentable as a sundered affair, and she was brief. It said, "Brock, it was great, but it's time to find the next galaxy. I'm moving to Colorado. Love, Renna."

Returning home early that day, I noticed how the snow softened the edges of the land. I studied the huge sycamore overhanging the 8th green from the side, guarding it like a dragon. Peering out, just then, the impenetrable gray sky, the underworld gloom felt oppressive and something seemed to shift inside as if an escape hatch had suddenly been glued shut. I kept remembering that part of Everett's diary where he received an anonymous message saying that he must leave the county or else, that he had done just that, though he later returned, in clandestine fashion, to rescue his wife Leah from a life of scorn and disrepute.

Maybe it was all in my mind, but I could swear I was being shunned and given the impassive look of censure all over town. Jeff Boggs scarcely nodded the week before when I saw him shoveling, and the amber-haired girl who worked at the convenience store, who had always greeted me and my steady trade in junk food with a kind enthusiasm, acted like I was on a work-release program. Even Nederland seemed to dodge me, having fallen into a clique with some other members of the cast. No one said anything about my equivocating part in the damn play, but there was nothing else that explained my suddenly becoming a pariah.

I didn't know what else to do on Christmas Eve, so I put on a tape of a thunderstorm with its cathartic percussion and lashing rain. When that didn't work, I began hitting the Dewar's. Laney was preoccupied with her upcoming performance and hardly noticed. She said she was going to drive over to the barn with the kids early to discuss some last minute snags with Joseph, and I could take the other car. By six o'clock, I was lurching around the living room like a pinball. The show was to start soon and, under the circumstances, the snowmobile seemed the most sensible form of transportation.

The effervescence of the dry, soft snow that fanned in my wake was more liberating than the jolt from the bourbon. I imagined Laney allowing me to take her for a ride, hurtling down the hills and flats of the golf course, her arms around my torso, her warm thighs clenching the rim of my own. I turned on the radio to the public station, and there was a folksy astronomer saying Venus was tracking around that night beside a sublime gibbous moon, but neither had yet edged over the pines. The host explained that the "star in the east," which the wise men were following like a pace-car was probably either a comet or an unusual convergence of planets. I confess I have always had trouble with the Magi. Following a star has always seemed as risible as accepting the opaque and equivocal directions of the heart.

As I tore across a bend in the terrain, the pitched outline of the shed came into view. There were a few small windows at the level of the loft. From that vantage and the heading of my approach, it looked like a ship in the middle of a night sea. I saw someone had rigged up a brilliant circle of bulbs at the zenith of the roof, with a cluster of smaller filaments descending and trailing away. It was not a particularly cold night and the stable door was left open. I could see the lambent glow emitted from inside, and also I could see a lone figure who was set apart from everyone else, removed from the recesses of the makeshift stage. My distant vision has always been exceptional, and at that moment everything seemed to have an almost surreal clarity. At first, all I could tell was that the isolated form was one of the Magi, but then I made out a crown and the distinct gestures of a man who was smoking. Even the way he held the cigarette, cocking it at a rakish slant, seemed affected, flushing it through his nostrils, so that his head appeared enveloped in a cloud. It was unmistakably Prevane.

The field was level now, and it was a straight shot up to where the cars were parked off to the side. The liquor had done its work, and though the speedometer read forty, which was nearly as fast as the machine had ever gone, I felt invincible. I suppose there was a fleeting concern about the repercussions of a crash, but those were submerged by the growing figure of my rival, like the words on the motel sign eclipsing each other in the same space. As I sped toward the entrance, there arose an epiphany that he had ruined my marriage and set my neighbors implacably against me. His name whistled in my ears like a demon's.

When the time came to hit the brakes, the transmission of that command met with strong interference and was superseded by the impulse to press down the gas pedal even further. It was the old problem of inertia, the difficulty of embarking in a new direction, strengthened by the counter tendency, after building up a little steam, to keep going for the far horizon. There are times when the exhilaration of swiftness can be a sort of ecstasy, and that must have been one of those moments.

Prevane, who was looking in at the rest of the troupe, rather than outward into the darkness, was, as it were, in my sights. As I took dead aim at the broad side of the rickety stable, the gentle lamplight that emanated through the wide door and seeped through the fissures in the wood made it seem translucent, incorporeal, a country mirage. For a second, I thought it seemed so brittle that there would hardly be any impact at all. There was only the wonderful sense of an unerring straight line, so rare a thing in the pattern of my life, toward the debauched psychiatrist suspended in the mouth of the barn.

Windhaven has a signature lighted ornament, which lines its streets like an occupying force, burning away our property taxes well into February because all the glitter seems to improve local sales. Those lamp post designs are comprised of a series of vertical strands, which taper at the sides and extend in the middle, below a wreath containing the image of a snowflake. In my delirium on the way to the hospital, I could not shake the nearly hypnotic suggestion that these shapes formed a replica of Everett's beard, and that unforgettable face seemed to appear and become luminous.

It was momentarily as if he were whispering, but I couldn't make out what he said, before the decorations became themselves again.

When I was released from the emergency room with splinters removed, shoulder in a sling and abrasions salved with ointment, witnesses recounted that the vehicle smashed through the back wall and lodged in a drift on the bank of a ravine. Laney decided she would hold off asking for an explanation, and after the doctors told her I was all right, she tried to make a joke of it.

"Your timing was impeccable. You arrived just after Fr. Gilroy said 'Peace and good will to men on earth.' Then all hell broke loose . . . ."

Mitch had gotten his cue a few seconds before my grand entrance, and was so oblivious to the sequence of events that he never questioned my intent. My version was that the accelerator jammed, and I was having an attorney look into it. Of course, the procession and mass, if somewhat delayed, went on as planned. Nederland later told me the wings on the paper mache seraphim flanking the altar were so large as to be almost menacing, and at communion he felt as though he had wandered into the aviary at the nearby zoo. Gilroy was in fine form for the sermon, getting a big laugh when he mentioned the drafty manger.

Now, three months hence, amid the inchoate edge of a new season, there are no undue residual effects except for a mildly sore elbow and the fact that our youngest son has to be repeatedly told not to run headlong into the side of an ottoman exclaiming, "Boom like daddy." Laney and I seem to have shaken the alter egos from our systems and regard each other generally with our original fondness. My wife, newly pregnant again, promised me she hadn't done anything with Mitch but complain about me a little, which I certainly deserved. We have decided to donate the staff, recognizing its dangerous power, to Mrs. Geiger for her flea market, where who knows what amorous havoc it may cause. Prevane, not long after wielding it at the pageant, was spotted being removed from the Mermaid Club—a local strip joint—after having lunged at one of the girls in her slinky aquatic gown. From what I heard, he just missed.

## *The Protectors*

Navigating the Winslow school gala at the Rhythm Club, Logan and Reese tried to seem casual, but amid the swirl of recessed lights and clamor of voices, they felt like they were entering the portal of a secret society. At the top of the steps, the Hacketts glanced around, as if looking for snipers and were not surprised that they knew almost no one. The room looked like an odd place for a fundraiser, a piano bar situated next to the multiplex, narrowly vertical like most saloons, with a curved bar and velvet ropes. Though the cramped space made the turnout look twice what it really was, the roaring 20's cabaret theme was a perfect fit. A jazz combo played a muted number designed not to draw too much attention. There were cigarette girls in confetti dresses that swished nicely when they walked, their fake packs of Chesterfields filled with chalky peppermint, and a guy in a long-tailed tux beside a prominent spinning wheel, its colors fanning like a peacock, for one of the raffles.

The couple maneuvered, as inconspicuously as humanly possible, to an empty spot. Fortunately, Reese saw a couple of the women she recognized from nearby Delmore Park where their lives would briefly intersect via children of similar ages. For a few minutes, under an arrangement of movie posters, they got caught up in some caviling gossip about the school's lunch menu. Logan tried to ease himself into their orbit, but there seemed something exclusive about the topic, so he relented and withdrew a safe distance where he studied their gestures and tried to lose himself in the general atmosphere. After that cluster dissolved, the two of them mostly heard fragments of dialogue that made little sense out of context, as if they were stranded in some foreign airport.

"I knew they would welcome us with open arms," Logan said over his shoulder as he angled toward the bar.

"Just try to blend in a little," Reese lightly scolded. "You look like you're about to get a tattoo in a sensitive area."

"Sorry, that's my default expression at these things," he said, snatching an hors d'oeuvre off a balanced plate before it bobbed away.

With their daughter Lizzie in first grade, after the forced hibernation of the preceding years, the Hacketts felt a certain restlessness to extend their horizons. Logan had been laid off six months before, and all the experts stressed that people were the key, not one's diplomas or experience. You were supposed to dive headlong into what was the neglected maze of neighbors, parishioners, and old classmates who knew you just well enough to mention another name. He should have been trying to inject himself into the fray somehow, but when he spotted Joan Kaufman, who had once cornered him looking for a commitment to coach a soccer team, he deftly guided Reese over by the stage.

They loitered there a while, but the trio had taken a break and with the music gone, it was like they had been deprived of camouflage. They quickly, too quickly, drank three glasses of wine, Malbec for him, Chablis for her, and moved into the warren of tables that comprised the silent auction. Most of the lists were not long yet and perusing the donated gifts seemed to carry the weightless, whimsical sense of thumbing through a tony catalogue or window shopping on Michigan Avenue. Reese must have had a revelation about the circumscribed life they led because her eyes popped when she read one of the items.

"Look at this. A week in a villa in St. Croix. Who here would have that to donate?" she said, keeping her voice beneath the hum of the crowd. There was a small picture and indeed it did look like some mini paradise. Logan's financial instincts, so much more finely tuned since his paycheck disappeared, kicked in. He scanned the minimum bid of $750 and for a second wished he could hide the zero. He noticed Reese looked great with some light eye shadow, jade earrings, and a long silky skirt that must have lain dormant in their closet since Lizzie was born.

"They can't be there all the time," he said caustically, also having been reminded of their present limitations. "What kind of sacrifice is it to donate the place for a few days? It's just showing off."

"Well, some total stranger in your place, in your bed, drinking out of your coffee mugs. It would feel weird," she half whispered, her gaze still fixed on the pastel veranda in the photograph. "It would be like inviting burglars in so long as they promised to put everything back."

"It's probably a time share, honey. Probably a regular commune anyway. No skin off his back. . . . Or hers."

They moved down the rows of prizes: dinners at steakhouses, Cubs tickets in the executive boxes, baskets of cosmetics from oddly-named boutiques, sets of fancy knives. He saw other couples stopping here and there to scribble the numbers they'd been handed at the entrance. Logan suddenly felt bad for his wife, tied to an architect relegated to making elaborate drawings of dollhouses for their daughter, weekends filled with inexpensive museums and Mediterranean take-out. He was tired of all the petty thrift that had entered their lives with the pink slip. With the loosening assistance of the alcohol, he seemed to move beyond some rather fuzzy breaking point.

"We may as well bid on a few things," he said nonchalantly, just as a woman screamed behind them when the spinning wheel skittered to a halt.

"We have to. These programs really help kids," Reese said, playing the sentimental card. "Shelly Brooks says her son Jackson is practically a chess grand master."

"I'm sure the Russians are shaking in their boots," he said, but Reese was already carefully writing their code, 147, onto one of the pads, tracing each number with a stone cutter's precision. It was then that they overheard a man at the other end of the long table, arms akimbo, talking to an older couple about "the islands" as if there was only one set and he was their magistrate.

"There's a tropical wind the natives call 'Marona' that comes up that time of year. But it's mostly a nice compliment to the sun. Good lord, don't go there if you don't like the sun," he said chuckling, his deep, honeyed voice easily traveling the twenty feet between them. He wore a pin-striped suit and kept twirling a pearl-handled cane, aptly depicting the role of a robber baron. Logan had seen him before, waiting for his son to be released from the "mad science" club, always chatting up the other parents with a particular kind of insouciant banter. "It would be a crime at that price," he announced, glancing at the low-ball initial figures. "The sunsets from the veranda alone are worth another thousand."

They left early because it was becoming too obvious, even in their near inebriation, that they were on the outside looking in, and Logan felt the babysitter's meter running like a cab stuck in a traffic jam. The cynical part of him knew that this was a way to score points with the P.T.A. since the night was young, and there were bound to be offers higher than the paltry sums they had put down. Their dog Bogie wouldn't be getting the full canine spa treatment and they wouldn't be acquiring the membership at Ridgetown Tennis, nor, of course, the splendor in St. Croix. Together with the entry fees, the safe bids had assuaged their guilt about so often remaining on the sidelines and there was something cathartic in pretending to spend money they didn't really have. Reese seemed rosy on the way home, probably with the notion that they had raised their profile in the community a little. There was a sense that some hidden upswing, embodied in the caprice of the evening, was not all that far away.

By then Logan was in full unemployment mode. He sent out resumes, took the occasional seminar on career "transitions," and was herded into the disconsolate job fairs. He still hadn't gotten used to changing roles with Reese, being the one free enough to pick up Lizzie from school when the peculiar staccato bell stridently sounded. It still felt surreal to be standing out by the north doors as the mothers and nannies lazily drifted in from all directions, converging at the edge of the building like automatons responding to some invisible cue.

He found himself hanging out with Dean Parnell, who worked a late shift at some security outfit, perhaps Logan's one friend in the neighborhood. They both liked to play softball and read, though Dean's interest ranged into science fiction, which Logan deplored. That weekend, Parnell was headed out to Aspen for a wedding he'd decided to extend into a rare holiday. He'd asked Logan to pick up his mail and move his car so as not to run afoul of the street sweepers and the parking tickets that ensued when you remained in their whirling path. He must have made an effort to make his apartment presentable before his departure, but this industry had not extended to his red '99 Lemans, which appeared as if it had been left somewhere to decompose and be reclaimed by the earth.

Nevertheless, the jalopy had all the security bells and whistles. By temperament, Logan had never been much interested in zealously guarding his possessions. He ridiculed the people with elaborate alarm systems as if they were no better than those who regularly predicted the end of the world. Even Lizzie was not immune to this nascent paranoia. She was currently in a phase where she fashioned elaborate traps so that stuffed toys would occasionally fall on his head when he entered her bedroom.

Before he left, Parnell took him out to explain the proper sequence to avoid triggering a siren worthy of the strategic air command. He handed Logan the remote control and demonstrated the buttons.

"If I forget, a Bengal tiger jumps out of the trunk or what?" Logan asked.

"No, that only comes with the deluxe package," Dean said, mindful that Logan was doing him a favor.

"I can understand all the precautions because this is a regular gold mine you have here." Through the window, Logan could see a pair of casually flung, dirt-encrusted sneakers, a laundry-sized heap of clothes, and an array of obsolete newspapers that were taking on a jaundiced tinge.

"It may not be pretty, but it's mine, and I want to keep it that way," Dean said, still buoyed by the idea of getting out of town for a while. "What about you? You think you're invisible or something?"

"It's a special talent I have. Employers especially," Logan said, always amused to spar with Dean. "I don't know why it hasn't worked with you. I must be losing my touch."

He knew Parnell, with his bachelor wardrobe and rootless history, was the kind of acquaintance Reese was rebelling against with her campaign to penetrate the opaque Winslow in-crowd. Many of their married friends had already fled to an outer ring of suburbs where they seemed as inaccessible as distant planets. They knew a few couples from church or Lizzie's playdates, but the connections were tenuous, not enough to feel comfortably settled. Logan had hung onto some of his single buddies as long as he could, but Reese had driven home how life with children was like crossing the Rubicon. "You might still be able to see the other side," she would say, "but there's really no way to get back there."

He had sometimes been reluctant to let some of the wild nightlife go, and he'd always been more comfortable with a kind of free-agent status drifting on the periphery of any social set. Yet without a job, he was determined to make Reese happy where he could and clearly that meant achieving some sort of acceptance where they had landed. These were the casual ties, which would lead to impromptu picnics at the beach and twilight drinks on someone's patio, with people who knew the crushing costs of children and accepted them almost defiantly. He had yet to fully change, which might require altering his DNA a little, but at some point he'd decided to join in her quest to get waves at the Farmers market or on a Saturday morning jog—to become included.

In search of other diversions, Logan developed the time-destroying habit of reading the neighborhood news. Jan Wetzer who lived in a townhouse across the street was the sole reporter for an internet paper called the *Sedgwick Loop* that kept him abreast of the controversies over a proposal to allow a Hooters downtown or some new ecological manifesto written by the president of the Garden Cooperative. One recent story seemed to have sustained a certain momentum, and the *Loop* was not about to let it die. Some oddball had been showing up at Hobson Park every once in a while wearing a superhero mask: Spiderman or Green Lantern or Optimus Prime, doing some one-man skit for the kids. There had been nothing particularly sinister besides the costumes, just a fellow from the neighborhood with too much time on his hands clowning around. Nevertheless, the parents, initially tolerant, had grown suspicious of the whole thing and had begun to form a posse. Someone had even gotten a blurry picture of the guy in a Phantom mask before he'd made his retreat.

Sometime in late September, when the gala had begun to fade into the oblivion of a thousand other awkward encounters, two significant charges appeared on the Hackett's Discover card, encoded to the point that their sources were inscrutable. When Reese got home, her face drawn from proofreading a stack of documents as thick as the *Gutenberg Bible*, Logan told her he thought their account had been hacked. "Look at this," he fumed, displaying the sheets of the bill across their chipped bureau. They had suffered an errant debit a year before and since then had been combing their statements like bank detectives.

"Oh my God. Don't you remember? Those are the amounts that we bid." Reese's mouth alone seemed to pass through several stages of incredulity and shock.

What she said didn't immediately sink in—it sounded like something from one of their occasional pinochle games where the currency used was matchsticks. Then it hit him, the glitter and velvet ropes, the feeling of being impostors and playing along to compensate. He focused on the much larger of the two, $900, the hazy picture of the cabana hovering somewhere on the edge of consciousness.

"You mean we actually owe this? How can that be? We were second on the list. That bid was just to boost the proceeds, to be good sports." He could tell that Reese was now suspended between desire and crushing restraint, that with the plane tickets and a new mattress they shouldn't have bought in the first place, there was no way they could do it. Plus, they had not heard a word about the prizes themselves; there was just the blow of the cost in their monthly balance.

They waited a few days to see if they would be notified about something, receive a festive card in the mail, but when nothing appeared, Logan resolved to call Winslow's front office to inquire, as gingerly as humanly possible, exactly what had happened. He assured Reese that he wasn't going to attempt to weasel out of it. They would be pariahs, laughingstocks like the plastered bum who had tried to take off with the collection plate at St. Alban's. Even if they merely sold the trip (probably at a steep discount given the short notice), Logan's connection with Winslow was a checkered one already. When he yelled for Lizzie to stop goofing off during her basketball practice, all outsiders were strangely banned about a month later. They didn't need another incident to cement them as oddballs.

The man who answered was definitely in the middle of some other issue, a child that had fainted or a clarinet that had been forgotten in a hallway. The best he could do was to give him the number of the lead manager, Mona Trill, who would be able to answer all his questions.

Logan had never liked such cold calls, nor the telephone at all really with its lack of visual context, its pauses that left you hanging in space. He'd had more than his share of intrusions, somehow having landed on a dozen solicitation lists. He was one of those old-fashioned types who would suffer through some poor sap's spiel before politely saying no. Even when they persisted for their chimney-sweep service or aluminum siding, based on the knowledge that many people could simply be worn down, he was gentle in the way he declined. So with the shoe on the other foot, when a woman's voice answered with a certain abruptness, he hesitated for perhaps a second, trying to arrange his words for maximum courtesy.

"Hi, the school office referred me to you concerning the silent auction," he said, with his most harmless inflection.

"Who is this?" she blurted, in a tone not merely suggesting a slight pique but outright indignation. It was as if this inquiry was either another in a stream of complaints she had absolutely no time for or she interpreted the slowness of his speech as the opening salvo of some anonymous deviant. Flustered, he again failed to convey his name and merely mumbled something about the fundraiser. The result was that she hung up with such force that the click seemed to convulse the delicate machinery of his eardrum.

It had been a long time since anyone had hung up on Logan. In fact he couldn't remember a single instance, even on a wrong number or during his tempestuous era of dating, when a girl named Anita once tried to run him over. Naturally, he was as annoyed as if he'd been slapped by a stranger merely for asking directions. But how else was he going to find out the specifics of what they had won?

He might have let it go, but he had always hated misunderstandings, the bane of the human condition, and felt sure she would effusively apologize once he identified himself and she could be sure he wasn't some lunatic stalker. He punched in the digits again, determined to be brisk, and not leave any dead air.

"Hi, this is Log. . . ," he said, this time with the proper sequence, but there was another terrible cessation of the line before he was able to get out the second syllable of his name. It was again like a small bomb had gone off at the other end. Now he was furious, especially when he reflected on how the club association at Winslow had so often been extolled as a paragon of civic duty. To be fair, all the rest of the parents he'd ever obliquely met had been very gracious. It was just his luck to have been referred to some descendant of Attila the Hun.

The lack of warning that he had entered into hostile territory vaguely reminded him of his firing, though that had at least been handled with some apparent remorse. Logan stewed about the whole thing in the confines of his bleakly quiet cottage, even going so far as to find a picture of Mona on the school website. She was not unattractive in an elaborate gown for a Mardi Gras night the previous Spring, though he felt he detected in her brittle smile a hint of malevolence. But, for the sake of his blood pressure, if nothing else, he mentally shunted the problem onto Reese's already full plate.

About three days later, the whole contretemps nearly evaporated when a letter arrived with coupons for Happy Companion where Bogie was to be manicured as finely as the grounds of Augusta National. A note from Max Kovalt on how to get the keys to his tropical duplex soon followed. Opening those, Logan figured the preemptive double hang-up would probably be placed in the massive mental file reserved for gratuitous insults that went unavenged. Reese had begun to dig in her heels on the trip, especially when she realized Bogie, after his celebrity treatment, was going to be more quaffed than she was. The smugness of Kovalt at the party kept coming back, how he seemed to avoid their eyes like they were homeless, how expansive he was with his operatic tenor.

"With Mr. Big doing his magnate impersonation, I was sure it would go for a lot more," Logan said, wading through his residual disbelief. "Maybe we can get half on Craigslist."

"C'mon, let's live a little for once. It's nowhere near the Bermuda Triangle if that's what you're worried about."

"Actually, I was a little more concerned about bankruptcy."

"Something will come through for you, babe," Reese said, her support still solid. "This is just a hiccup. We shouldn't have to shave our heads and pass the alms bowl in the meantime." Being as helpless as he was about securing their future, Logan wanted, as best he could, to cushion Reese from the present, give her a little borrowed respite in a faraway place, help her build a social cocoon to hold things together.

"We'll find a way," he said, with as much fuzzy reassurance as he could summon.

Out to move Parnell's car again, Logan failed to turn off the force field or whatever it was, so that the chassis lit up like Times Square, and a signal shrieked wildly until his stabs at the black gadget in his coat suddenly made everything fall silent. Jammed between a van and a Honda, the decrepit vehicle had to be angled back and forth to clear the bumper. Something in the back kept distracting him, so that after he'd gained the new spot, he crawled over the transmission column to get a better look. Being all mixed up with a collection of other junk, it hadn't been obvious, but as he felt the rubber texture, a mask's features emerged out of the mess. Despite having little familiarity with most of the comic book heroes, Logan guessed it might be Captain America but it could have been Thor or the Incredible Hulk or any of the dozens of fabulous creatures the studios kept churning out. Turning over more of the stuff, he found a few more painted with brilliant colors he couldn't place at all.

It was obvious Parnell had to be the guy who was going over to Hobson Park. Logan remembered he'd seen Dean's Super Shield company truck on the street a couple of times, and that it had several of the muscled icons surrounding a logo that said "The Protectors." Dean had probably gotten the stuff for some promotional shots and decided to have some fun. Caught up in the fantasy books he was always reading, he probably imagined himself that way, keeping everybody safe and sound.

A couple weeks later, there was a monster tornado about a hundred miles away in Claremont that demolished every structure in its haphazard path. Perhaps influenced by a teacher who'd lost a relative to one down south, Reese got the idea to set up a hot chocolate stand outside Lizzie's classroom for the victims. By then, Reese had already been swept into the bleeding-heart tides of the Winslow fraternity: arts councils, food drives, crusades against overmedicating the slow learners. She seemed to have passed through some subtle barrier and didn't mind the consequent rush. They had even gotten invited to a party or two that before had required some password like at the slot of a speakeasy.

The morning of the disaster relief, when Logan looked for their car in one of the accustomed locations, it gradually became clear that it had disappeared. The police were called, the insurance company notified, and he rehearsed in his mind a response to Parnell whose suggestions for better locking devices had been ignored. Reese was obviously dismayed but mostly seemed to center on the callousness of the timing. She had taken the day off from work and just finished the ominous curling lines depicting the maelstrom on a piece of cardboard. There was the ten-gallon container and a dozen boxes of mix, the hundred cups and stirrers to transport by two o'clock. Logan told her she could take Parnell's car while he hurried to the store for marshmallows, which she had belatedly determined were critical to the project's success.

By the time Logan arrived, sweaty from jogging with a grocery bag, Reese had just finished setting up the table with one of the volunteers, who as she came into focus, constellated into the wanted poster of Mona Trill. She looked a bit different from the photograph, her hair thrown across her forehead, the rise and fall of her long legs now outlined in the woolen stockings that had become so fashionable. The school gong was due to sound any minute, so there was no immediate option for reprisal or escape. It was galling to see her in this supportive role, the sight causing some powerful dissonance that seemed to be located somewhere in his throat. He would have preferred to limn the whole of her without any redeeming quality, demonize her with a broom circling the vortex of the downstate storm. Fortunately, she was just heading back inside with some empty boxes as he arrived, merely noting him from a distance as a member of the crew.

"Lovely car Dean's got. Does he live in it?" Reese said, as a multitude of small children, the ones let out a little early, converged.

"Well, he's something of a barbarian. But I think he's one of the good barbarians."

The expanse of park behind them, with its backstops, goal posts and soccer nets, marked a congeries of sports totems that made the broad view of the place seem confusing and alien. The bored crossing guards and games of tag were present as always. Lizzie and her classmates held up the crudely-sketched sign advertising the cause. A giant thermos was on one side of the table along with the cashbox and the various ingredients were strewn across the rest. Reese adjusted the cloth they had draped over the whole facade to make it look more like a booth.

The weather seemed perfect for this kind of sale, cold enough that the warmth of the drink was desirable but not so chilly that standing out there for an hour would be like the last leg of Everest. Gusts of November wind, perhaps remnants of the colliding pressures that had flattened Claremont, occasionally whipped the hoods of their parkas. Logan noticed Max Kovalt, wearing one of those designer sweatsuits, as he pushed his son on the swing so hard it seemed the kid might be launched over the slides.

A rogue gale almost took a box of spoons over the side, but Logan lunged and caught it at the last second. "It looks like we're having a 'Marona,' he said, the word having stuck in his mind.

"What?" Reese said, overwhelmed and trying to smile as a mob coalesced in front of her.

"Never mind."

There was something beautiful in the flurry of youth suddenly released from the bondage of fractions and geography, except that a part of the burst was now aimed, like Pickett's charge, at them. Already a line had formed that extended beyond the threshold of the playground. Reese was preoccupied with getting the hot water into the cups while Logan tossed stirrers into them and took the proceeds. They kept trying to economize the process to move things along, the hasty pouring of the packets growing increasingly haphazard and off target, but it didn't seem to matter. The turnout was shockingly good, and every time Logan looked up, the line still zigzagged to the edge of the climbing wall.

Reese was beaming at all the business, as if she could feel her stature in the school ranks ascending with each smoking drink, and even Logan was not immune to all the positive vibrations that swirled through the gathering. Maybe this simple sacrifice would improve his image in the neighborhood, too, redeem his unemployment and the series of clumsy remarks he seemed to utter in every random social situation. For the first time, he even allowed himself to relish the trip, how the sands of the Caribbean would be like a balm for their pummeled nerves. But the main thing was that Reese was happy and they were no longer some remote couple on the fringe.

After about twenty minutes, at least three dozen parents remained arrayed in loose huddles, shifting on their feet as the queue slowly advanced. Mona reappeared standing at the edge of the action, talking with Jan Wetzer. Logan couldn't help but feel that Mona was appraising him, though she couldn't have known he detested her, that it had been his voice on the other end of the phone. He felt safe having his true identity hidden, and it reminded him of those trick windows where you could see out and yet remain obscured.

Lizzie, the putative sponsor of the whole enterprise, finally reappeared from wherever she'd been playing, but Logan immediately saw she was wearing the Phantom mask, the one that had been featured in the *Loop* story. He quickly realized she must have found it in the backseat of Parnell's car and stuck it in her backpack. It was a bit on the creepy side with its grotesque nose, arched eyebrows, and garish smear of a mouth. Reese squinted but nothing registered amid all the smoking liquid and bills being passed.

"Take that off, honey," Logan said, hoping to deflect the whole thing as a joke. "You might scare away the customers." This remark only served to draw more attention, and he heard the group that had formed around Jan and Mona erupt, someone even pointing Logan's way, as if he had sprouted horns or brandished a pitchfork. Mona's gaze didn't waver as she digested the familiar visage of the mask. There was a commotion amid a gaggle of women bunched near a platform, such that their expressions seemed to morph into a tribunal. A moment later, some disturbance spread across the larger audience, as if the first notes of a dirge had been piped into the courtyard.

"What's going on?" Reese whispered, a study in bewilderment, as parents began guiding their children toward the parking lot, the few stragglers grabbing a steaming cup and tossing payment quickly on the table.

"It will be okay, honey. We can just explain the whole thing," Logan said, holding down all the flimsy Styrofoam containers lest they get scattered by the turbulent billows. Logan tried to maintain an outward calm, but a part of him was suddenly livid that they could all turn so swiftly, without a shred of evidence that Logan and Reese had done anything wrong. He mused that maybe he would steal a rare ashtray from the villa, which might finance the whole journey; that perhaps he would sabotage

Mona in a manner she would never be able to trace. Defiantly, he thought that the insurance from their stolen Saturn would be better than the piece of junk itself and that next week there would be a juicy job offer in the mailbox. He thought that before long they would find safe haven like when the sky sometimes softened and seemed to embrace you with its shelter and all this unpleasantness would pass.

Lizzie must have been feeling left out because she undid the creaky latch on the old, gunmetal cashbox so that it flung open wide, exposing its ethereal contents. Unfortunately, this impulse happened to coincide with one of the peculiar rushes of wind, such that a large pile of the hastily stuffed bills flew out in a green cloud of money. It was as if a flock of tropical birds had gotten spooked and all lifted into the air at once. Then the cash was tumbling, darting, sailing to the far corners of the park behind them. A cry rose up among everyone that remained, and though his legs felt weighted by stones, Logan found himself already giving chase, as if his life depended on it.

## *The Waiting Moon*

Jarrett wakes with the disorienting sense that he has missed something, that there has been some lapse and he must try to figure out what's gone wrong. Passengers are wearily lining up in the aisle, jostled by the accustomed roughness of the old rails. The street and buildings out the window are upscale, mildly forbidding and unfamiliar, especially when compared to the ones he has headed past a thousand times. Dusk is shading the sky and the whole thing has the feeling of a hoax, as in the movies when the villain slips a tranquilizer into the detective's drink. The train is slowing down, clamoring into some anonymous depot.

This disconnect hasn't happened since he was a young man, when sleep would come upon him like an irresistible temptress, even with the prospect that he would keep going and going into terra incognita. He wonders if he has been snoring or worse, muttering nonsense, which Blair insists he sometimes does, yet with the demeanor of someone completely lucid. Somehow, he has hurtled four or five stops past his own, straight into the secluded, clubby territory of the North Shore. It is as if he has crossed a border, passed without fanfare into another country. He hurriedly grabs his monthly ticket, raincoat and valise, and now sees from a small sign he has landed in Kingston.

The station is one of those quaint, square buildings with carved wood benches that was probably erected in the thirties. There is a chalkboard listing the cost of snacks in a florid script, along with a drawing of a cup of coffee, its wispy smoke caught in a spiral. There is a framed map of Midwestern routes, an antique clock with Roman numerals, and a rack of faded books that have been offered to pass the time. Everyone who disembarks the 5:49 trudges up from the culvert where the tracks lie, forty or fifty steps to the level of the street, probably rushing straight for home.

Of course, Jarrett is annoyed with himself for having overshot the target. Now, he will have to head in the opposite direction, backtrack over the same real estate, which has always felt like the most obvious confession of error. If he had not let the syncopated rocking of the car lull him like a hammock, had he taken out his laptop to check the market returns or the latest global calamity, he would now be pushing the door open to the subdued welcome of his collie, Porter. Blair is out of town at a convention, but he would have his leather chair, his paintings, his comfortable refuge.

Yet there is something vaguely pleasant about being where he doesn't belong, a spy behind enemy lines. It has been ages since he and Blair have gone somewhere new on vacation, allowed themselves to be surprised. Studying a schedule on the counter, Jarrett sees that the next train into the city, running against the outbound tide, won't come for another hour. He contemplates a cab, but that would cost a sawbuck and who knows how much sooner it would arrive? Jarrett has always been curious about those affluent suburbs running along the lake—Hillbrook, Indian Grove, Waterside, Newport—but for a long time he has had no real reason to explore them.

There was only the one year right after graduate school when he had serendipitously lived on the edge of all that. He had met a rich girl and for a while was carried away. There was a certain atmosphere to that string of places on the shore; cloistered almost, cut off from the straight, main roads, with huge lots as if etched out of a forest, cobblestone streets, the feeling that there might be some quaintly preserved ruin underneath. Then, he returned to the middle-brow places, the surroundings of his youth, as if he had never left. It was like a sabbatical, a rare detour from actual life, though he couldn't have known that then.

Jarrett heads outside before even realizing he's decided what to do, perhaps spooked by the station's sense of abandonment. The town center is prosperous but spare. Though it's almost March, spectral white lights still limn the young trees along the parkway. He strolls past rows of boutique shops for flowers, photography, southwestern artifacts, and trendy clothes. No bar, no oasis of commuters lingering over a drink presents itself. He supposes that the shore crowd doesn't want riffraff from the city, him included, trekking up here hoping the money might rub off. Even the lake itself seems bluer and more serene the farther north you go. It all fascinates him because he knows it's as out of reach as a mirage, a picture in another dimension.

Finally, Jarrett rounds a corner and spots a bookstore. Its lambent glimmer signals that it has not yet closed. A small bell clangs as the door shuts, and a woman nearly obscured by a stand of titles studies him.

"Welcome, but I must tell you we're only open another forty-five minutes," she says, halfway between apology and announcement.

"That's fine. I'm just . . . ." He is about to say "killing time" but then realizes this would too bluntly betray his situation. "If that's the case, I'll try to be decisive."

Jarrett surmises this is the kind of store that relies on a personal touch, no alarm system at the exit, and the woman probably acknowledges every customer. A dying breed. The chains, with their branded codes on every piece of merchandise, their security guards, and banal selection of authors have all but taken over.

At first, he feels like a tourist, that sense of being in a bar where you don't know a soul and are under inspection. But the woman's voice and the pleasant ambience of books quickly dispels that notion and makes the place seem the sort of hideaway he seldom discovers. Jarrett's needed something new for a while but couldn't say exactly what. He wonders if the shop is just the sort of find that could nudge him out of his recent ennui.

In his 44th year, this malaise has descended on him stealthily, out of nowhere as they say, its source eclipsed. Though it seems to have something to do with Blair, with some subtle erasure of life before her, as if he'd lost contact with all that had existed before they met.

Jarrett slants toward a shelf of paperbacks. He knows he will have to buy something now, with these independents slowly edging toward extinction, the woman's approach a kind of plea. She has retreated to the register to ring up a purchase for two teenage girls who keep giggling over some private reference. Jarrett remembers how that morning, when he went to pay for a croissant, one of the dollar bills had a cramped note written in ballpoint pen that said, "Feast of St. Anthony, patron of lost objects. This is your lucky day. Soon, you will find that elusive . . . ." Then the goddamn space ran out. The cashier had stared as if it were counterfeit but eventually placed the note in the drawer with the rest and that was that.

"Could I help you find something?" the woman asks quietly, almost as if they were in a church. She is only a few feet away now, having crept up so silently he is a bit startled, thrown out of the paragraph he has been trying to follow.

"Oh, maybe," he says, as he recovers his bearings. He wants to tell her of his predicament but decides it would be too complicated for such a straightforward question. "Do you have any good biographies?"

"Sure, they're on the other side." She makes a vague pointing motion but doesn't finish it before maneuvering around the stacks that rise almost up to the tile ceiling. Her hair is a sandy blonde, styled nicely with the kind of curl that wraps around at the bottom, and her lipstick is almost undetectable, a shade of pink. He can sense her passion for books the way she holds the thick volumes, surveying their covers and the kind of paper inside, running her fingers across where she has randomly opened it—a sort of muted reverence. She is small, ethereal almost, but not delicate somehow.

She has a gravity like those celestial objects that have weight without the proportionate mass. Only then does he notice the nametag: *Rina*.

"There are some good new ones on Samuel Johnson, Whitman, Nelson Mandela, if you fancy any of those," she says, clearly soft-sell, knowing what an idiosyncratic choice it is. She keeps an arm's length between them in the tight aisle. When she reaches for the spines of the ones she wants to recommend, she does so without hesitation, as if she has memorized their bindings. There is a certain roughness in her tone that dismisses any impression of intimacy. She is not distant, merely self-contained, turned inward, as if she were in two places at once.

There is so much in a voice that can captivate or repel him. Beauty has always been his weakness, not wealth or fame or even happiness. Nor does he have to possess it. Just being near beauty is often enough, quietly marveling at it, a spectator. In a flash of uneasiness, Jarrett senses he knows her from somewhere. This impression seems nonsensical, yet cannot be easily dismissed. The feeling is more like some element in the space around them, not altogether in his power to banish.

She excuses herself with an air of impatience as the phone rings, again the old-fashioned sound. Jarrett tries to restrain himself to the sort of meandering peeks, which would be expected in any such scene, occasionally pausing over some oblique view as she leans into the desk—the stylish pleated skirt, the not too pronounced arc of her calves, the unaffected pose. Jarrett is sure he's never been here, but the store carries a similar echo of reminiscence, not déjà vu exactly but more like an affinity, a homecoming. It's odd how often this happens, some fleeting displacement, such that he can no longer picture the location of his flat, the vase in the vestibule, the view of chimmneys from his office.

The walls have elegantly written passages from some novel or other set unobtrusively in the corners. It is as if he has entered a sea of words, which circulate through some imperceptible ether in the room. He passes a man with a leather jacket that has an eagle on the back, perhaps the logo for a brand he's never heard of, a designer's idea of what might be in vogue. Its talons, are poised to grasp something below, are curved like scythes.

Jarret decides on the Lindbergh bio, picked almost on a whim so he has not wasted Rina's time. Wandering over to a bulletin board, he sees a notice for a book reading by an author named Charles Severn. After a double take, he recalls that he'd once read a novel of his, which for a while had enthralled him. There was something elemental about his work, but as with so many things from back then, he cannot recover the title or even how it ended. It is yet another aspect of his life that has been largely jettisoned in the rush of adulthood. Jarrett decides he must get back for this.

To Rina, who has again wandered into his area, he says "I remember him." He motions toward the tacked-up notice. "But what's his most famous one?"

*"The Waiting Moon."*

"Yes, that's it."

Jarrett is seized with the compulsion to see if he still has it, though he suspects the volume was donated to a church sale long ago. The title alone seems imbued with another era, in that way hearing an old song will catapult you decades back. Rina, too, has begun to take on the buoyant cast of those days. There is something in her expectant manner, out of the valence perhaps, between people who find they share the same fascination. She seems almost coy for an instant, stretching her arms behind her, suddenly lit from within. They walk back to the computer, and, after searching the antiquated machine, Rina finds that the book is out of print. She offers to check if there might be a stray copy floating around. "You never know," she says, with more hope in the idea than it seems to deserve.

"Sure, when you have a chance. Do you know anything about his new one?"

"The reviews have been so-so, but I'm still eager to hear him." Perhaps out of some reticence about revealing too much, her gray-green eyes dart to a display of staff favorites, with personal comments beneath them.

"Yes, I'm going to come back. I've only seen pictures of him." As he says this, he drifts toward the entrance, not wanting to delay her closing up shop. For the first time, he senses her appraising him, perhaps to probe if he is sincere, whether he really will return. He reflexively brings a hand to his cheek because a few years ago there was an accident that required some minor surgery. It had come out well, although everyone knew that some plane of his face had been altered. He'd grown a close-cropped beard to mask the change and kept it ever since.

"You should. It will be interesting."

Just then, there is a commotion, a pounding on the floor, which is so exaggerated by the previous silence as to seem like a mortar attack. They both turn to see the man with the flamboyant coat running out with an armload full of picture books. Rina remains frozen while Jarrett lurches after him, a beat too slow, rattling the feeble bell. Jarrett barely gets outside before giving up the chase as hopeless. Slightly winded, he returns to see Rina steadying herself against the counter, not even calling the police. Suddenly, something in that particular version of her profile, the way it seems stripped of emotion, reveals who she reminds him of. Neve. Lovely, haunting Neve. Another thing he has forgotten but not quite. Rina is older, of course, but in this light almost a replica.

"I'm sorry. If I'd seen him sooner . . . ," he tells her, a bit deflated at this exhibition of his physical limits.

"Don't be. It just caught us off guard." A bit shaken, she looks up briefly, with a mixture of regret and gratitude for his having been there, if only as a witness. "Every few years that happens. I guess no place is immune."

He is about to ask if there's anything else he can do, when a man close to her age, late-thirties perhaps, wearing a paddy cap, enters the store and speaks to her in a familiar way. Jarrett pretends to be tempted by a row of coffee mugs, an excuse to linger. This interval is simple curiosity, he thinks, the innate desire to fit pieces of experience together, make them comprehensible. He takes in the man's shock when she relates what just happened, but the exchange is hushed, and Jarrett can only speculate what is said from the body language. There is no embrace, just a brief pat on the shoulder, yet this gesture could still hold a host of meanings.

Jarrett avoids the conductor's eyes on the way back, relying on the fact that he could not possibly keep track of the attire of every passenger that has come aboard. He doesn't feel he should have to pay an extra fare for travel that he never wanted, even if the result now seems fortuitous. When he succeeds in evading detection, this escape generates an outsize relief, as if he's just engineered a heist at Sotheby's. Jarrett pens a note on his portable calendar for the reading and mentally pledges there must be no excuses, no allowing this event to be submerged by the distractions of his usual circuit, no convincing himself later that nothing really happened.

Jarrett remembers he won't have to call Blair to relieve any worry about his lateness. She acted like it was a nuisance having to go to San Diego for the firm's glitzy meeting, but it seemed to him that this pretense was for his benefit, and there was some part of the trip beyond the amazing weather that she looked forward to. Before she left, they'd had a small argument, and he wishes now he'd left it alone. Blair had just changed the message on their phone recorder to "Anything you say can and will be used against you, but be a sport and leave one anyway." He took the direct approach and told her that despite the joke, the subtext might be off putting. "Your attorney friends will like it, but what about everyone else?"

Finally home, he hears Porter whine in gratitude. The air of the condo seems oddly compressed, as if it has been shut tight for weeks. Jarrett is happy to have nothing else to do but cook himself a quick omelet, one of the few dishes he can safely manage, and watch the travel show on the public channel. Over the last six months, he has tried a Tai Chi class, a seminar on Cartesian philosophy at the junior college, and hikes in the nearby forest preserve, but none of those activities has really intrigued him. He has almost resigned himself to the notion that he'll never be completely bowled over by anything again, get that illumination that seems to reconfigure the world.

Blair has tried to reach him at 6:30 when he would normally have been home. After getting a glass of Sherry, he returns the call, and when she answers, he can already hear a rush of disparate sounds—the hum of static, voices, a tangle of instruments—in the background.

"Oh Jarrett, it's crazy," she half shouts. "Give me a minute. It's like a riot in here." As he hangs on while she steers herself away from the noise, he thinks of the few colleagues she likes, all women except for Ben Stalls who is portly and not her type. To his knowledge, neither of them has cheated, but she occasionally accuses him of flirting, which he does not deny outright. Jarrett has always considered this fair game, "*Joie de vive*," in small doses, as long as it doesn't go too far. But later, he feels guilty, as if he really did something.

"Okay, I can hear myself think now," Blair says, suddenly out of the blankness of the connection.

"Whatever you say can and will be used against you."

"That's been my assumption since I was a little girl . . . . How are you?"

Jarrett considers whether he should tell Blair about his little adventure, eliding the dangerous parts, but lets the urge pass. The bookstore isn't the kind of place he could bring her because it is as still as a cathedral. What he finds peaceful, she judges to be slack, a sensory deprivation chamber. He is still in love with her, but after twenty years it is a static love, and there is no such love on earth that can compete with an unknown one, the blaze that never goes out. None of this is Blair's fault, his sense of being hemmed in, the enervating routines. He finds great comfort in their meshed lives; rounds of dinner parties, the cocoon of family.

"Fine. There's something to be said for a little solitude."

"If that's the case, maybe I should stay another month or so." It is hard to tell over such a distance, over the crackle on the line if she is a little hurt or being playful or both. He understands this jab to be just another facet of the marital tug of war, the attrition of little disagreements, like a tide eroding a coastline.

"No, please don't do that. By the time you got back, I'd be muttering to myself, talking to imaginary friends."

When she cheerfully agrees, he's again tempted to tell her of his day, but even with the drink he can't quite get there. It isn't some dark secret he stealthily withholds, but it would be hard to convey over the phone. There's no way he could make her understand, without raising suspicion, that he doesn't see the lapse now as a blunder at all, something more like fate. He recalls a quote from Joyce, "Mistakes are the portals of discovery," and feels as if a previously concealed gate has swung open.

Blair begins some vague reply, but the line is abruptly cut off, and Porter looks up suspiciously, as if he were the cause.

Passing his stop again, Jarrett feels a surge of anticipation, a sense of being flung beyond his customary orbit. As he watches the yards grow larger, the houses more opulent, Jarrett thinks of that scant piece of summer with Neve in this genteel district, how the woman and the landscape seem hopelessly intertwined. He'd sublet an apartment from a buddy who had decided to go into the Peace Corps. It was the best place he'd ever lived, maybe because he knew the whole arrangement was ephemeral, due only to a series of fortunate accidents. It was only a hundred yards from the train station, the sounds of locomotion during rush hours regular as a watch.

There was a small theatre across the street whose marquee announced only art films that were hardly being shown anywhere else. The apartment had a diagonal view of an oddly affordable French bistro called "*Trois Facons*" that hosted eclectic ensembles on weekends. It had a fleur-de-lis motif at the cornices of the building and a scalloped winerack behind the bar. Despite the fact that her family was rich, Neve worked there as a waitress.

Jarrett could never forget the long black apron, falling to her knees, over a white shift underneath, that comprised her uniform. There was something about the contrast and fineness of the strings, the perfection of the figure-eight loops, like a butterfly almost, tied at the base of her spine. She was slender, feline, dark haired, olive skinned, always with a touch of smoky eye shadow. There was a reserve, an uncommon grace about her, some observant, hidden quality. She had even chosen to go by her middle name, her real one remaining a secret he'd never been able to pry loose.

Jarrett doesn't recall things in a linear way; it is more moments, sometimes the smallest images shunting aside the seminal ones. They all drift back in their own languorous way. Neve's house had twin cupolas making it seem like a medieval fortress. To be in the spaces they created was almost like being in a separate compartment, floating, disembodied. It was all so new: the sprawling mansions, the country clubs with their long driveways and inner precincts, the jetty near the canted masts in Bishop Harbor, the small dunes near Conner Beach where they would nestle and watch the circling gulls. Jarrett remembers how Neve had been shocked at his thrift store furniture and then charmed, like they were stowing away in a boxcar. The whole affair had only lasted two weeks, but, being summer vacation, he had seen her nearly every day, and the episode had left a lasting impression.

He eventually heard through the grapevine she had become involved with someone named Hugo, a guy she met when she was abroad in Spain. There had been a sweet but terrible note. He thinks now that it was like she'd been stolen, like the picture books in that entirely unforeseen alteration of the way things had been a moment before. When she disappeared, if it was something he said, there was no outward reaction. The judgment occurred at a remove, in a separate place where reasons need not be given. For a while after, he dated many girls but not for very long so that they tended to blur into a montage of dizzying nights. He had kept her in his mind for a year or two, but eventually he could no longer hold vigil for the loss.

By the time Jarrett arrives at the bookstore, the reading has already begun, so he gingerly eases himself into a seat in the last row of folding chairs. He scans the room for Rina and at first does not see her, but then does, in a tiny café arranged in an alcove. Her head is tilted, resting against her hand, and she has one long-skirted leg wedged against a stool. From that vantage, she doesn't seem to resemble Neve at all, and he feels momentarily idiotic, that he has made it up in some strange vacancy of his heart. Then she shifts and notices him, lifting her eyebrows almost imperceptibly, and the presentiment of Neve suggests itself again, though the whole effect is more equivocal this time, as through some maddening screen.

Severn wears a black pullover sweater and has a shock of unruly hair falling off to the side. Almost immediately, he does not seem quite right, swaying at the podium as if his balance were impaired, and the cadence of his speech is uneven. By the third paragraph, it's clear that he's had too much to drink. Severn reads a few passages of the new book and they seem good if not exceptional, although Rina appears to be completely absorbed, pondering every phrase.

After a few minutes more of his erratic performance, Severn acknowledges the thin applause, almost dropping his glasses in the process. Jarrett is determined not to ask him about *The Waiting Moon* or the long hiatus after, as he supposes that this creative drought must be part of what is driving the author to distraction. Yet, a few others are not so circumspect and come right out with it. Severn tries to keep a polite veneer but doesn't quite manage—a slight shaking of his head, the jaw tight as a violin bow, a flush rising.

"That was so long ago . . . another life," he says, deflecting his discomfort with a joke. "I was a different person then. Weren't we all?" The audience, perhaps sensing some condescension, seems restless. One elderly woman reaches for her purse and discreetly withdraws. Probably to ward off the lull, Rina raises her hand and extravagantly praises the excerpt he has chosen before asking about his influences.

After Severn has scribbled his inscriptions in the sold copies and shared a rueful laugh with Rina, he leaves quickly. The store has nearly emptied, and she rubs her eyes as if she is very tired. Jarrett thinks of the other man, the one with the cap who clearly knew her, but there is no trace of him. He sees her take a sip of wine and light a cigarette, though he's sure there's a ban in the village. He notices the bottle on the counter has a fleur-de-lis emblem and remembers the French restaurant. It comes to him that it also had writing on the walls, although he had never translated the language. Rina scans a sheet of purchases with the somber air of someone reading the obituary of a distant relative. The shop must be on its last legs but like her reaction to the theft, she's good at hiding her feelings from a stranger.

"I shouldn't have gotten into this business for love," she says.

Jarrett wonders if this comment is a reference to a relationship or the place itself. For the first time, he notices she wears no ring, though this means little anymore.

"Yes, I'm afraid the barbarians are at the gate. It's not a good time to be anything but gigantic."

"I have a lead on getting a copy of *The Waiting Moon* if you're still interested," she says, gently stubbing the half-smoked cigarette out on a plate.

"Yes, that would be wonderful. Just to see that book again. Like bringing back an extinct species."

"The source wants to remain anonymous. I hope you understand."

"Even better. Just a wink and a nod."

"Do you mind my asking what it is about that particular book? I'm this way myself sometimes, just having to have it, despite everything." She takes a long sip of her Bordeaux, savoring it, holding it on her tongue as long as she can.

"It's quite a long story, but I guess the short version is that I'm one of those fatuous people who can't relinquish his youth. I know the facts but they don't seem to matter."

"So you are like everyone then," she says, with a hint of a sigh.

He thinks to press her if they can continue the conversation somehow, see where it will lead. A few days ago Jarrett never would have thought himself capable of stepping over that line, of creating that kind of havoc.

He pauses as if suspended on a wire, considering how he could phrase such a question so that the intent was not so obvious, the suggestion not so clearly drawn. But he has delayed a beat too long, and she begins to gather up the papers.

Jarrett has to grab his coat, which he's left near the makeshift lectern and after retrieving it, he finds that she is leaving, too. There is still another forty-five minutes of light, and with the limpid sky, it feels like darkness is even farther off. After a slight hesitation, they both find themselves heading east, and Jarrett adjusts himself to her more measured pace. They make small talk but just moving beside her makes everything take on a surreal aura, like this convergence were just some scene being reenacted in his mind.

They quickly get beyond the business district and walk past an impressive church whose intricate stained glass window glints like a benediction from the descending arc of the sun. Then, it occurs to him that they have taken a different route and are only a block from the place where he had once lived.

"I'm sorry. I must stop here," he says, when they get to the old building, with its ochre brick and marble cornerstone. It takes him a little while to take in the sight, hold the ordinary façade against all the ghostly flashes he has carried around inside.

"Is this where you live?" She says this with a strange inflection as if she already knows the answer. She looks up and then spins around to take in everything that is there and not there anymore on both sides of the intersection.

"No, in the city. But I did live here a long time ago."

Again, she displays the wrong reaction, not as someone would register a fact but rather confirm a hunch. She seems perplexed, amazed, bemused all at once. "It's a lovely street," she whispers, almost to herself.

The French restaurant has been replaced by a series of shops: a realtor, a Yoga center, an investment firm. The theater is still there, though slightly less dilapidated than he remembers. He took Neve to a few movies at the art house because she was a cosmopolitan sort, craving the enigmas of the foreign. From his small den, he watched the marquee change from week to week, the lines becoming bigger and smaller, the neon streaks tracing a pattern along his mantle when the curtains were pulled away. Sometimes they would go over just before the feature ended and listen to the reviews people gave as they streamed out into the night.

"You should go up," she says impassively. "It might bring something back."

When Rina leans forward a little to focus on the upper floor, he spots the smudge of a birthmark at the base of her neck. Though this imperfection merely verifies what he already knows, a current rushes through him, seeing this part of Neve that had transfixed him, a kind of fingerprint no two women could have. Rina is the name she would never tell him. Her hair and clothes and make-up have changed but almost nothing else. Jarrett sways a little and can no longer picture where he really lives, how Blair moves nimbly through their comfortable warren, the dim contours of his actual existence. He wonders if it is the same with Neve, one world having to efface the other.

"No, I don't think they're home."

This time she does not deflect him; she looks and looks as if her eyes alone could explain everything, with that expression she had of inevitable retreat, of being drawn toward some inaccessible room. "I really must run. Hugo will kill me if I'm late again."

He catches a sliver of the lake between the trees a mile down, feeling suspended where no movement, forward or backward, is possible. He wonders why he has never tried to track her down, make contact at least, just to see where things stood. Then he realizes it would have been like searching for a revenant of what she was, of what he was, when everything that mattered had yet to happen.

"I guess I'm like poor Severn, trying to pick up where I left off," he says, finally allowing himself to regard her again. Jarrett sees the flutter of her scarf, the tossing of curls across her forehead, the way she clasps the belt of her coat, as Neve sometimes did, the images somehow converging.

"It's an odd feeling," she says shyly. "There but not there. Gone but not gone."

"Yes, exactly."

"Well, goodnight," she says softly, with her heels already clicking on the sidewalk, then half turning with a wave, a fleeting motion almost over before it begins. Jarrett gazes up at the set of windows and without the glare sees crescent shapes, perhaps some ornament hung from the ceiling like wind chimes. He suddenly recalls what *The Waiting Moon* had been about; some repository for the splits in the road, a place for all the things that never quite had a chance. He remembers the book strewn across Neve's lap one evening after she had fallen asleep. A streetlight flickers making a strange reflection on the pavement. She is just a blur on the horizon, but Jarrett traces her outline to the point of vanishing. He watches as a lithe young woman ties a narrow, black apron behind her, somehow able to weave the straps where she cannot see them, from memory.

## *Last Shot at Vader*

At last, Dillon and Riley get their tickets under the already beating sun, while thousands of other lightly clad tourists swarm through the turnstiles. Especially the day after Christmas, Dillon knows there will be countless more lines to come. He is not good at waiting, regardless of what he brings to distract himself and his daughter will have to be diverted somehow, as they inch their way to the exhibits. Still, just being with her as they enter the park seems worth the whole trip, this fantasy village drawing them into its elaborate mirage. Riley is so entranced at the explosion of shape and color, the wonderful strangeness of the winding streets and arabesque roofs, she seems to hardly breathe. A giant mouse eared billboard asserts "Disneyland-The Happiest Place on Earth." This claim strikes Dillon as an awfully ambitious one but for the moment, with Riley beaming at the spectacle of it all, he isn't about to argue the point.

Maps in hand, they wind past the series of 19th century New Orleans shops where a man in a striped suit plays a lively ragtime. By nature, Dillon is not a planner, an itinerary guy. He likes to think of himself as versatile and spontaneous, even though this is mostly a cover for random and haphazard. Incredibly, there is no line for the Enchanted Tiki Room, and a woman in a Malaysian get-up is beckoning to fill the hard seats of her show.

"How about this, Riley? It's like an island place."

"Will we have to take a boat?" His daughter is inquisitive, with longish blond hair perpetually flying around, somehow amazingly strong without any apparent muscle, and given to the nonsequiturs of a seven-year-old.

"It's a magic island so we can just walk there. Nothing to be afraid of."

Riley has been a bit frightened of water travel ever since a ferry ride they took to Victoria when he and Kim were still married. Across the Strait of Juan De Fuca, it was harrowing, the craft tipping to a thirty degree angle at one juncture, surrounded by nothing but waves. Dillon dearly hopes neither this nor the divorce has made her more reticent somehow, left any lasting imprint.

For once on this joint vacation, Kim has reluctantly surrendered Riley's company to meet with some old school chums and have a few uncensored laughs. Oddly, the three of them are staying in the same mediocre hotel, The Eldorado, inhabiting rooms on opposite ends at double the cost. All the Spanish architecture, juniper trees and endless news of droughts and wildfires reminded Dillon he wasn't in the Midwest anymore. At one point, after a solitary stint at the meager lounge, he got disoriented and almost walked into a neighboring suite, which could have led to nearly any reaction from mild shock to gunplay.

Inside, there are brightly-plumed wooden birds on the walls and three huge ones in a giant cage at the center of the hut. Exotic painted totems gape from posts and ledges throughout the theater. There is a brief introduction by a middle-aged man in a long-toothed necklace and an outfit fashioned partly from straw. He does his best to create a sense of drama, but even with the background fanfare, there are traces of his weariness, the monotony of the speech he has recited so many times before. He suggests in the manner of a subtle command that everyone remain in place until the exit signs come on. Riley is rapt and sidling up to Dillon on the bench, so he can put his arm around her, making Kim's remoteness and the considerable turbulence he encountered over the Rockies to get there all fade away.

When the show begins, he is not quite prepared for the volume of the singing parrots, macaws, and cockatoos, the startling way they move their massive beaks and feathers, for the medley of gongs and flutes, the flashing bursts of tropical light. Riley may be a little spooked, but she is mostly taken by the way they harmonize with perfect pitch and rhyme like Dr. Seuss. The opening rendition of "In the Tiki Tiki Tiki room" is suitably tame, and they all clap as the equatorial atmosphere suffuses the room. The next number, "Let's all sing like the birdies sing" is so hammed up, with the central players twirling their candy-bright tails, Dillon finds himself hitting the predictable notes along with the rest. But then there is a distinct change of mood, descending bamboo shades all around plunging them into darkness. This shift is followed by a thunderclap, a volley of drums, and the illusion of an engulfing rain. All the sound effects lead seamlessly into some kind of foreboding war chant.

Perhaps it was all the coffee Dillon had gulped that morning to compensate for the slack hotel mattress, but after the first few bars, he feels the specter of his lifelong claustrophobia returning by degrees. After another minute or two of the amplified percussion in that sweaty, cramped row, he is practically jumping out of his skin. His attention veers away from the avian emcees toward the thatched perimeter, but the doors have melted into the shadows. Something about the performance carries him back to the ship from hell and the tempest that had come up. Dillon grabs Riley's hand and makes his way out the narrow aisle, along the back of the tent to where he remembers the signs. The man who had made the introduction, grass skirt and all, materializes beside them, motioning toward a corridor behind a column of leering masks.

"Somebody sick?" he whispers, not without agitation, beneath the cacophony bombarding the stage.

"Yes, emergency, I'm afraid," Dillon says, tilting his head toward Riley and hoping to convey some bodily mandate that requires immediate evacuation.

"Okay," the man says, indicating a nearly invisible exit, constructed entirely of hay, without handle or demarcation. He opens it only a crack and urges them through, back into the brilliant morning.

"It wasn't over, dad," Riley says, with a mixture of disappointment and complaint. Yet, this response seems more muted than it would have been a year earlier. He has noticed that she treats him with even more affection than before the split, perhaps because he isn't involved in the day to day squabbles, or simply misses him, though she never puts it that way. For his part, he is careful not to force her into the emotional acrobatics of choosing sides.

"We'll catch the end next time sweetheart," he says, trying to hide his relief at getting out. "I'll make it up to you."

They walk to Tom Sawyer's Pirate Lair where Riley keeps ducking into tunnels too constricted for Dillon to enter, beyond which a hoist brings up a treasure chest and then a full skeleton whose boney hands are unable to release it. Then, there is Tarzan's Treehouse whose winding staircase makes him clutch the thick rope holds as if he were dangling over a precipice. Fortunately, King Arthur's Carousel is next, and then they take Mickey's monorail that circumscribes the grounds and forms their boundary. From this perch they can get a glimpse of the big picture, the fairy tale spires and bastions, along with the nomadic herds of people migrating through a network of clogged channels.

"How's school going, honey?" he asks, while they are aloft, glad for a reprieve from all the Bedlam.

"Pretty good I guess."

"Just tell me one thing you found out lately. I never get to . . . ." He starts to explain the simple revelations he's being deprived of but doesn't want to burden her with any of that angst so he trails off.

"The hippocampus is where information is stored," she shoots back with pedagogic authority.

"Wow, that's great, sweetheart." He is consistently amazed that already Riley knows about topics that are beyond him, even if they are mostly of the sort which would only be useful on a game show. "You're really getting smart."

"But I don't want to be a genius. Einstein's brain got so big it exploded. I read it in Captain Fact."

"I don't think that's what happened, honey. He could have hit his head or something. Maybe Captain Fact should change his name to Captain Doubtful."

Dillon is tempted to ask her about her mother's new boyfriend, but he refrains, again not wanting to make her part of the caustic struggle between them. Kim is seeing Wayne, a large man who wears suits and has a roaring laugh, details Riley has offhandedly confided before. She seems to view him as overly solicitous, which makes Dillon picture him as a stock broker wooing a big client.

Dillon well knows the upheaval of a household split. His own parents had been divorced, largely owing to his father's wild streak, which often found him seeking the excitement of his army days in a far tamer place. There were the periodic bar scuffles and gratuitous acts of bravado, and the sense of never knowing what stunt he might pull next. One infamous incident involved him diving into Lake Brentwood from an awfully high bluff, leaving the family to wonder for fifteen long seconds whether he would ever surface.

Back on terra firma, as Riley studies a wandering mime, Dillon feels the unpleasant vibration of his cell phone, which reminds him of one of those prank buzzers that would jar him as a kid. He knows it is Kim checking up.

"How's everything going?" Kim asks, unsuccessfully trying to keep her concerned edge out of the question. She is calling from the Getty museum where she is meeting her friend Mariel who has a split-level in Malibu. Kim hates amusement parks for some reason, maybe similar to the way some people can't stand clowns. They have done a few things together—Santa Monica Pier, Grauman's Chinese Theater—subduing the usual friction, but this is her day to decompress.

"So far so good. I think Riley wants to build her own cartoon house and lived here for a decade or so."

"You're staying as close to her as the Secret Service?"

He has been given a paper with every bit of Riley's identifying information conceivable. She's wearing a florescent jersey, designed for bike riders, due to the early winter dusk. Kim had even wanted her to be equipped with pepper spray, but he managed to scotch that precaution as being over the top.

"Absolutely. Everything short of a leash." Dillon could hear Kim sigh, begin to issue some retort, and then let it go. He corrals Riley over behind one of the kiosks, so as to block out the whoosh of the waterfall ride and a calliope somewhere in the background.

Dillon has a hard time explaining where he and Kim went south because there was no single incendiary event, no smoking gun. He supposed the rupture circled around the notion of temperament. Whereas she was originally drawn to his cool, analytical persona, over the years she gravated to a more adventurous type, someone less governed by trade-offs and second guesses. He could see the change in her choice of movies, in flattering remarks about her friends' husbands.

Dillon figures things began to unravel when Kim started watching the weird cable shows. Despite his absolute fidelity, she regularly tuned into *Cheaters* and *Who the Bleep Did I Marry?* where private eyes catch bigamists and swindlers and charlatans with odd fetishes. No doubt her friend Penny Birkdale was behind this whole kick. Penny suspected her husband Jeff of having something on the side, but Dillon didn't think anything had been conclusively proven. There were the usual conspiratorial conversations. Kim must have reasoned that betrayal, like most everything else, was contagious if given the right conditions to bloom.

"Are you sure you can make it all day?" she inquires, disparaging his fitness with that same corrosive lack of confidence he knows only too well. "Maybe I should come back early."

"I think I can handle a little walking around at half a mile an hour."

"Hey, don't forget about the pictures, all right? That's half the fun."

He has never understood the photograph craze. It just seemed to replace the actual experience and store it in some future archive. Kim had lent him her fancy camera, probably a gift from Wayne. But gadgets tended to baffle him, and her thirty second demonstration seemed like a review of the cockpit of the space shuttle.

"Don't worry, Kim. I'm on it." He watches Riley take pains not to spill her Yosemite Sam Taco all over the place, her neatness another new development. "Are you admiring sculptures that don't resemble anything in particular?"

"Can I talk to Riley a sec?" She completely ignores his joke, maybe just trying to speed things up so as not to abandon Mariel too long. But Dillon still feels the sting of being a mere conduit to the one she loves, as if he were holding their daughter hostage.

While they chat, Dillon lets himself think about the stupid quizzes Kim would sometimes have him take. For a while, she would subject him to a different personality test every other week, to see which character in *Lord of the Rings, Downton Abbey, or Game of Thrones* he most closely resembled. The questions followed a certain pattern, and there was always one or two that gauged one's appetite for risk or romance. He would usually fall into the clever-friend category, with very little of the warrior stuff. As asinine as the appraisal was, he knew this bothered Kim, that perhaps she had expected him to fight harder for her. Dillon wondered if she would have changed her mind if he had tracked Wayne down and taken a few swings at him, even if this only served to land them both in the emergency room. He'd had a few choice words with the interloper, but by that time the whole matter seemed *a fait acccompli*. And wasn't that the modern trend, to settle your differences with a peace conference or a trade of prisoners? Wouldn't the choice of blunt force over negotiation just earn you a restraining order?

The Finding Nemo Submarine Voyage is out of the question so they opt for Mr. Toad's wild ride, which is not terribly wild and Sleeping Beauty's Castle, which makes him drowsy. There is Alladin's magic carpet tour and the Little Mermaid's swishing tail, which, for reasons he doesn't want to explore, seldom fails to get his attention. Tomorrowland and the Sorcerer's Workshop, two of the attractions high on Riley's list have logjams that he cannot withstand so he ushers them to the less popular Monsters Inc. diorama instead. She does great in Splash Mountain with its plunges and spray; there is no hint of panic beyond his own jangled nerves.

By three o'clock, Dilon feels the excursion has been a limited success. Riley is enjoying these fantasies but both of them are getting lethargic from the heat and running out of things to say. Dillon is tempted to make an excuse, head to a restaurant with sun umbrellas and call it a day. But he knows Riley may never get another chance here and isn't ready to go, that he needs a few more rides to erase his blunder in the Tiki Hut. There are other places Dillon wants to be able to bring her back in Wisconsin—the race track, the Ringling Brothers Museum, the Dells—and if a memorable tour through this onslaught of Philistines is required first, that's a sacrifice he is determined to make.

As he returns from somewhere inside his head, there is an instant when Riley isn't next to him and not in any of the frames his vision darts across. Even the piercing note of dread that enters his voice is swallowed by the hubbub of the crisscrossing mobs. It is as if his heart has stopped as he whirls in every direction, but when she answers back "Over here" she's only a few yards away, partially obscured by some sort of Roman pillar.

"Riley, you've got to stay next to me," Dillon says, a little out of breath, his pulse trying to find its rhythm again. "We're together like there's a string between us, okay?"

"You sure worry a lot, dad"

"My doing that kept you out of harm's way since you were a baby, didn't it?"

"Maybe or maybe I'm just lucky."

"Well, let's not test your luck anymore today, alright?" he snaps at her misplaced innocence, but he is too relieved that she isn't lost to pursue it any further.

She is standing next to an oval stage and a sign beside it that announces "STAR WARS PADAWAN TRAINING—NEXT SESSION IN THIRTY MINUTES." Riley nods but is clearly transfixed with the message before her, the idea of this intergalactic instruction. She has long been fascinated with soldiers and pirates and ninjas, more so than the girly stuff, anything with hand to hand combat. Dillon thought this interest went a bit too far, blaming Kim for enrolling her in Tae Kwon Do when she was still in kindergarten. It is just another example of how he has allowed Kim to steal Riley away a little at a time. Perhaps the class just clashed with his pacifist instincts and the notion that for all the toughness his father had, none of it had prevented a semi from veering into his lane on highway 42 one night and killing him instantly.

"Are you sure about this, Rye? There's plenty of other stuff on the other side."

"That's okay. I need to learn this." Without any further consultation, Riley sits down cross legged at the base of a platform with her Mulan book, clearly ready to wait until midnight if she has to.

Dillon would love to get a drink from the concession that is just a stone's throw away, but the area around them is gradually filling up, and he can't ask Riley to risk her spot in the front row. He opens the park brochure with its miniature atlas. Like any foreign map, he cannot really grasp it, the compass points, the convoluted lanes are all but indecipherable. When he finally decides they will just wing the rest, he looks up and sees a woman in a large bonnet make an abrupt stop and peer through her sunglasses at them. She is holding the outstretched hand of a young boy who seems to want to get loose.

"Dillon Burke?"

He is terrible at recognizing people from his past, has always been slow to call back a name but with her, out of the blue it comes to him. "Grace?"

"My God, I can't believe it. I never figured I'd run into you again." She bends down for an awkward hug that he tries to reciprocate without tipping her over.

"Like the sign says, small world," he manages to say, pointing to the marquee for one of the exhibits.

"Not exactly the same thing," she responds, quickly turning and grazing his shoulder. "Have you been in there? Kind of creepy."

"Riley wants to see the *Star Wars* thing. Since she saw that sign, the rest of the place sort of disappeared." Dillon turns to get Riley's reaction but there is none. The kids are eyeing each other, Riley poking the boy's helium balloon in the shape of Donald Duck.

Dillon knew Grace at Kensington College where they had sometimes run in the same gang. She was a genuine beauty, had reminded him a little of certain actresses, the modulated raspiness in her voice, the brooding mystery. He thinks how she is striking in a different way than Kim, smarter in a way that remains largely veiled. While Dillon plotted how to approach her, another guy, had swept in like a marauder. Grace wears a long flowing print sundress patterned with a geometric design. Some caprice of the breeze intermittently limns her subtle figure. He recalls hearing that her marriage hit the rocks a couple years back and as far as he knows is still living in Chicago.

"Who's your friend?"

"Riley. Second grade. She says she wants five doctorates. I guess I have my work cut out."

"This is Roy. Spy/detective/tennis pro. Depends on the day."

He moves to create a small space on the concrete beside them with Riley in between as a buffer.

"Who's your favorite Jedi Warrior?" Riley bluntly asks Grace.

"Gosh, I guess I don't have one. It's been eons since I saw this."

Riley's face goes blank, her wariness of Grace seeming to ratchet up a few notches. "My mom likes it when they fight. She practically jumps out of her seat."

"You're right, honey. That's when she used to spill popcorn all over the row in front of us," Dillon says. He's meant this as an innocuous anecdote but again Riley clenches her jaw, annoyed that he would portray Kim as clumsy, reveal a gaffe to an outsider.

When Grace notices Roy clutching his trousers, she flashes her winning smile, and holds her lovely arms up in mock surprise. "Be right back," she says, ignoring Roy's protests and shuffles him toward a bathroom. Dillon can't help but watch her deft movement around the curve of the path, the gentle cadence. His renewed dating has mostly been comprised of a series of mini-disasters. The dodged kisses when he dropped them off, the clashing politics, the probing questions for which there were no good answers. Lately, he feels like a punch-drunk boxer nevertheless propelling himself back into the ring. But Grace's reappearance has had a magical effect, generates a transcendant ray of hope.

"Who is that lady?" Riley whines. "Isn't it supposed to be just you and me for a change?"

"Sure, honey," Dillon says, feeling the full weight of so much absence. "As soon as the show's over."

A flurry of activity at the edges of the small amphitheater signals the cast has assembled, strutting, already in character. The get-ups and strobe lights are all first rate. There is never a moment when Dillon thinks he's wandered into some fly-by-night neighborhood carnival. When the theme starts up, Riley is already in one of those spells that displaces one reality for another.

Like a lot of things in his childhood, he has forgotten how caught up he'd once been in the *Star Wars* craze, how the more menacing elements haunted him, the nightmares of princesses abducted and planets obliterated by a death ship. He now remembers the makeshift capes, the headbands drawn from rags, the swords fashioned from a score of objects of similar shape. Vader had come on the scene just when Dillon's parents were going their separate ways. There was a time when he had embodied all evil in his sinister image, the perfect vessel for malevolence, everything that was wrong with the world.

A young tag team with form-fitting jump suits and microphones sewn into the collars alternately explain how only the children who are chosen get to participate and everyone else must stay behind the ropes. There is a sternness in this decree that conjures up how crucial it is for the apprentices not to get separated from the guardians, to avoid a stampede, the possibility of a kid wandering off amid all the confusion. A long, rectangular fountain blocking the stage like a moat seems to reinforce the necessity of the audience staying in place.

The real ringmaster, Han Solo, jogs out center stage followed by mute stormtroopers that have been gathering in bunches on the periphery. Han describes the whole business of what it means to be a padawan, the initial phase of becoming a Jedi knight, and exhorts all the children who are interested to raise their hands. Riley does this so timidly, Dillon is sure she will be rendered invisible, but somehow Solo rewards her restraint. Dillon coaxes her to walk up to where the others are being sized for the brown, hooded robes and handed plastic light sabers.

Grace and Roy return, twisting themselves through the tight sections of onlookers. "Even the bathrooms are disguised," Grace says, rolling her evocative eyes. "He didn't appreciate the Tinkerbell motif." Being just a preschooler, Roy doesn't seem to perceive that he's missed out on anything due to the untimely call of nature. Dillon is close enough now to notice Grace's mild scent, a beguiling amalgam of mint and hand lotion.

"Riley got picked," he says, with more excitement than he intends to reveal.

"Oh, goodness, there she is." Grace stares, mouth open, and eyebrows raised. "They won't have a chance against her."

It's a nice family scene, the kind Dillon has not had in a very long time, and he finds himself lingering over the intricacies of this beguiling woman's expression, the contour of her elegant cheekbones. He watches her dig into her beach bag and emerge with a camera. With a shooting pain in his stomach, Dillon realizes his own has remained buried in his backpack. He scrambles through the sunblock and flip-flops and granola bars to the small device, and searches for the proper buttons.

"Don't worry, there's still time," Grace half whispers, patting him lightly on the knee, her touch setting off a visceral jolt. She seems charmed by Riley, taking a few shots of her even though she is just a blur with the other cadets. He has a sense she isn't really in a relationship anymore, like him, just managing the fallout from the last one. Yet he considers whether he could withstand the blast of another rejection just now, if he will take his usual path of least resistance.

The trainees are directed to spread out in the oval encased by the audience. Solo begins teaching them how to use the weapons, the release that opens them, the swiping movements and thrusts that will be needed in their duels with Vader and Darth Maul, his terrifying ally. Riley is very intent during the tutorial, studying every facet of the stance and grip. Dillon watches her reverently handle the sword. For a minute the mechanism catches in its sheath, but after another try, springs out.

With the blare of a few processional chords, Darth Maul and his minion ranks, the droid soldiers, stride down a designated path into the cordoned ring. He is painted all over with cryptic symbols and wields a double-tipped crossbar that simulates some pulsing destructive power. The padawans are being lined up along one side of the stage so that they can individually climb the steps to do battle. Then with another crescendo and clouds of smoke, Vader rises majestically on a platform in the middle of the proscenium. Just as in the movie, he is hypnotic, somehow eight, maybe nine feet tall under the flowing cloak, the unearthly, amplified voice, the impenetrable visor.

Captured by the thrill of this presence, he feels a prayer forming that Riley will be able to figure things out in a way he never quite has, be able to hold her own against these macabre villains. He knows he must get a tremendous picture to make up for all the ones he's missed. It won't be one of those bland everyday photos you see plastered all over Instagram, but just the two of them, Darth on his heels, parrying her blows, retreating from this tiny whirlwind. It will be an icon, something you could frame and tell stories about forever.

Roy is in Grace's lap, riveted by the ominous chords of the Imperial March, Vader's signature breathing, his scripted invitations to join the dark side. "It is the only way to save your friends," Vader bellows, taunting the crowd. The system is that each kid gets maybe thirty seconds in the spotlight, each time fighting to a draw, then they are steered back down to where a separate group sits on the ground. Grace turns to Dillon, with an unabashed smile the likes of which he has not received from a woman in ages. He feels transported as if time and space were not ineluctable laws but something that could be shifted around, backward and forward.

Dillon clutches the camera in a ready position so he is sure to get several views of the skirmish. But when he peers over to the ascending line, he doesn't see Riley who should be slowly edging up to the front. With a bolt of disbelief, he recognizes her being guided away with the ones who have finished, who in their clustered robes now resemble a gathering of monks.

"Oh no, no, no," he shouts loudly enough that everyone in his vicinity can hear, even over the concussive notes of the song. He immediately apprehends he hasn't blown Riley's moment—there has been some mix-up of the lines. "They screwed it up," he continues in a furious growl, only meeting Grace's stricken eyes for a second. He rotates to see Riley gazing back, palms up in a gesture of bewilderment and resignation, and it is as if he has actually been stabbed someplace inside where the blood remains hidden. Dillon tries to signal her in code, waving with idiotic and indecipherable motions, that she should get back in the procession that leads to the duel. But she has already been herded into the other camp.

"Oh, that's a shame." Grace tries to console him even if the only means at her disposal is empathy delivered with a look of exquisite softness. There is a moment when it is all too much, the phony psychological profiles, the million goddamn plans which go awry for no reason, the whims of fate. For once letting himself be pulled into the eddy of pure impulse, he is on his feet, dodging a column of engrossed patrons, ducking under the rope. Dillon practically shoves one portly gentleman who is lodged in the only viable path to the aisle, which keeps shifting like a current.

The stormtroopers, who have been making antic pratfalls, attempt to remain in character as, with robotic movements, they order him to stop. When he ignores them, they begin to surround the kids, cutting him off from Riley. Dillon has no choice but to jump into the reflecting pool, getting soaked to the ankles, wades for a couple strides and stumbles out at the base of the footlights. He can see that she is frozen, unsure whether to beckon him closer or urge him to go back.

In his thunderous drone, Vader is now adlibbing for everyone to remain calm, that the "intruder" should report to the service tent. "Your thoughts betray you," he goes on, almost seeming to enjoy this departure from the tedious script. When Dillon fails to comply, he changes his tactics. "It looks like someone does want to join us . . . welcome." His voice has risen an octave higher as he tries to humiliate Dillon into submission. He can hear a few in the crowd begin to jeer, and Solo is by then looming with some actual security who are not wearing funny costumes. They have him all but encircled yet seem hesitant to proceed, not wanting to disrupt the show.

Through the pandemonium, he spots Riley again and for once she is cheering, consumed in that rare approval she so often bestowed before their lives fell apart which even across the chasm feels like a warm embrace. Dillon wants to get to her, gather her up and hoist her high above everyone so she might never be overlooked again, but the only passage is hopelessly blocked by a roiling sea of strangers.

Beyond the point of no return, Dillon's only route of escape is up a ramp that must be there to move some of the heavier props. He knows it isn't Vader's fault that he didn't get to see Riley more, that things didn't work out with Kim and never even got started with Grace, that an oncoming truck lost control on a desolate country road, but it doesn't seem to matter. He catches a glimpse of Grace huddling with his daughter, probably trying to convince her this turmoil was all somehow part of the act. Once on stage, Dillon would never be able to say whether it was some survival reflex or merely the chance to get one last indelible shot at Vader. He picks up a toy blade that had been dropped amid the melee, raises it, and charges after him.

## *Home & Castle*

It had been six months since Drew was laid off from his job as an analyst for Rimland Containers, and already the notion was growing that he could be stuck in that limbo for the long haul. His lingering resentment made it hard to keep up certain social pretenses. The sober habits of professionalism ingrained over the years—the six-thirty wake up, the unwrinkled shirt, and close shave had almost completely fallen by the wayside. It stood to reason that gym shoes and a worn flannel shirt would suffice when he didn't expect to see anyone except a clerk at the pharmaceutical counter or a neighbor walking his Malamute. People cut him some slack in the beginning, gave him time to absorb the blow, imbued with the knowledge that catastrophe was often without fault, and, on occasion, wholly random.

But appearances mattered and empathy had a fleeting half-life. After a while, the initial support of Drew's friends seemed to be morphing into an unspoken indictment. Some of his more distant acquaintances took their aloofness further and seemed to be calculating how long it would be before his and Zoe's nest egg ran out. He'd gotten so that he could detect the faintest slights, though they were often so rapid and ethereal that he usually failed to note them in real time, only feeling their mild sting as the encounters unspooled later in recollection.

One February morning, Spike Davenport, who Drew routinely chatted with at the beach last summer, stalked right past him with barely a flicker of eye contact. That he was buried in his cell phone like a lover, like this was the hotline to Beijing was hardly an excuse. Everyone knew that the gadget was one's first line of defense if you didn't want to talk to someone, if you wanted to be encased in a cocoon of self-importance. People now used them to ward off undesirables as effectively as a taser or pepper spray. This was just another small cut, but he felt it keenly, like the slashing wind off the lake.

Drew was on his way back from one of the thousand errands which seemed to spring from the vacuum of his new condition. The store was only about a mile away, and he did whatever he could to replicate his former route from the train, which despite its punishing sameness, awakened some nebulous feeling of purpose. In front of a nearby three-flat, he saw

Carol the postwoman in a rumpled blue parka wheeling her stuffed sack of envelopes. He knew her name only by the tag on her vaguely military shirt, but they had exchanged a few pleasantries when crossing paths in his building's vestibule.

As he approached, she seemed to be ensconced in the frigid solitude of her journey. On another day, Drew might have nodded hello and kept going, but he saw fewer people who wouldn't render some veiled judgment lately, and it occurred to him he might lighten her load by taking his combination of bills, solicitations, and flyers a little early.

"Good morning," Drew said, in his most sanguine tone. "Can I just take my mail from you now? It might be easier."

"I beg your pardon?"

He thought she might have misheard him as the gale had whipped a real estate sign planted on the lawn as he spoke.

"I just thought I would save you a trip," he said, adjusting his hood and as he did so, grazing his brittle, five-day beard.

She straightened up as one accosted and clearly not recognizing him out of context, said, "Sorry, but you could be the man on the moon for all I know. I'm supposed to put it in the box." The expression on her face was akin to someone who had just dodged a potential flasher as she ambled past. In his pique, he came close to yelling that she wasn't much improvement on the Pony Express but it occurred to him that a stretch of unemployment could even change one's features, like the distortion that often appeared in a mug shot.

Fortunately, Zoe remained firmly in his corner despite the setbacks, though at times he detected in her a certain wistfulness, as if she felt the scope of her dreams contracting. Her freelance illustration business, sporadic as it could sometimes be, was keeping them afloat. But it was hard not to feel something more than money had been left behind along with the sprawling factories and spreadsheets at Rimland. The disparity in their relative usefulness had upset some arcane marital equilibrium. While Drew headed off to the grocery store, bank, cleaners and the community thrift shop to jettison piles of obsolete toys, Zoe embellished websites, often going to people's homes.

Recently, she had been hired by an elderly spinster who was trying to sell oven mitts decorated with fascimiles of cave paintings. "Don't let Maisy talk your ear off," he might say, as she departed. "There should be an extra charge for having to hear about her parakeet's latest adventure."

"Can you run to Mattigan's and get a new bathroom faucet," she would reply, ignoring his attempt at a joke. "The water is coming out like a fire hose." Apart from his time answering want ads, the sum of Drew's intellectual powers seemed to have been reduced to the items in a checkout line.

The loss of general station he felt had just begun to intensify when Drew got an email from Martin Langford, a friend from their time at Tranmore, a little-known private college in Ohio. Martin had been the golden boy, blazing through his honors business classes, landing a spot on the corporate ship even before he had donned a cap and gown. He was built like a greyhound, well-trimmed, and had an enviable store of charm. Drew had lost track of Langford, except for the occasional mention of his colossal residence on the south shore.

He and Martin had never been that close and yet the esprit de corps which emerged from being in the same fraternity made them friends of a sort. Nevertheless, a boozy misunderstanding the night before graduation had opened a breach, when Martin's loaded girlfriend enveloped Drew in a clingy embrace for a photo. Langford had wrenched her free, seething "Nice try, Brutus," the house's standard term for a traitor, before whisking her onto the dance floor.

But Drew was glad that the contretemps, its edge eroded by time, had blown over. The email was breezy and informed him of an alumni outing for dinner and a play downtown. Martin had signed the note "Hoping you'll be there for a few laughs about the old days." It showed his title of Executive Vice-President for *Home & Castle*, a tony furnishings franchise, in elegant script at the bottom.

Theirs was an instantly recognizable brand name, a symbol of upper-middle class taste. It was where brides-to-be were registered for wedding gifts and new homeowners browsed to fill the compartments of their expanding lives. The price of the reunion seemed way out of bounds, and besides Drew wasn't up to the evasions that would be required to hide his pitiful circumstances, so he politely declined.

It wasn't long after, that Zoe got a call from the referral agency for a three-month stint designing the background of a catalogue for *Home & Castle*. Usually she was ambivalent about the potential gigs the headhunters sent her way. Often they either involved a halting eighty minute commute or were as dull as a coal mine. Yet this assignment was altogether different, and Zoe was thrilled at the prospect of working even temporarily for the company whose products she had been drawn to even as a child.

After they'd finished watching one of those BBC detective shows they'd become as addicted to as sunshine, Zoe suddenly opened up about what the job would mean.

"It's just perfect. Three months, enough to show them how I can draw. Then we could still go to Glen Arbor for the cherry festival." Her sister had a cabin in the Northwoods, and they were both desperate to get up there, as if their troubles only resided in a single location. "If they like me, maybe it would become full time. God, I think I would design some of those cool plates for free."

"Let's not get carried away," Drew said, surveying the sagging and otherwise decrepit furnishings which surrounded them. It was only Zoe's considerable artistic skill that rescued the drab living room. Her flair for capturing a face, the expectancy of a pet golden retriever, the unique lines of a waterfront lent their meager home an air of low-key style. Drew had considered dropping Langford a note to see if he might provide her with some advantage but disliked the idea of exploiting connections and figured she deserved it on her own.

"The bright colors and oddly practical shapes, the cute knicknacks. They make you feel you're already half way to the Caribbean."

"If there's any justice left, you'll get it," he said, regarding Zoe's smooth complexion in the soft lamplight.

They still had a few pieces from a decade before, obtained in the flush of a new condo, but several had been chipped or simply disappeared, casualties of everyday life. When Zoe bought a set of baskets from the nearby outlet as a shower gift the previous year, she'd nearly broken into sobs at the register. Drew didn't know if this reaction was because they were so beautiful or because they were for someone else.

Drew had to concede the cleverness of their trademark, with its allusions to the protection and grandeur of another age. But he was fairly well impervious to their commercial magic. He had long avoided malls and department stores as just another form of traffic jam. They seemed to represent everything that was wrong with the country, the guise of tranquility masking the avarice that was flogged in every aisle. The shopping centers even occasionally gave him an odd form of vertigo. If he were forced to pick up some item, the way the exits were hidden would make him feel trapped. A sensation would came over him of standing on a boat, the only thing beneath him the pitching floor of a running current. But he wanted Zoe to be happy and tried not to dampen her enthusiasm.

"It would be great," he said. "Replenish the coffers and hopefully by then, I'll have rejoined the real world."

The day of the interview, Drew had a session with his life coach Clifford at the local café, which made a superficial attempt to seem like a rustic hunting lodge. Drew had begun that service when it became apparent that he was going to be laid off and decided on a few more appointments after the axe had fallen. With a steep discount due to a friend's referral, he wasn't about to forego the counseling when he seemed to need it most, when he felt as adrift as an astronaut whose spacewalk had gone awry.

Clifford was waiting in a booth near the back. He was sure Cliff only had a masters in psychology and some bogus certificate, but Drew liked him anyway. His name and the fact that he had a huge head covered with ruddy locks never failed to evoke a book Drew had read to his daughter Nell a hundred times about a giant red dog who played havoc with his normal surroundings.

Outside an awning flapped and strained from a mid-winter gale before receding in exhaustion. The fake fireplace in the center of the room seemed a source of comfort, not unlike some immemorial hearth, even if its flames radiated no real warmth and were as unvarying as the burner on a stove.

"Hi Drew," Clifford greeted him, though his attention kept returning to the *Sentinel's* sports page. "It's like the North Pole out there. Get a warm beverage so you can thaw out."

"Don't mind if I do. Will the meter be running while I languish in line?"

"Of course not. But watch out for those muffins, a zillion calories. That wisdom is on the house."

It was a measure of how comfortable he was with Clifford that he hadn't bothered to change out of his customary tramp costume—jeans that had seen better days, a jersey, sneakers, and a coat with a balky zipper. He knew it was a kind of passive defiance for those not prepared to move off the grid or burn a tuxedo. The experience of being cast out from the norms of society had aged him, with gray unmistakably infiltrating his temples. It was amazing how a few months out of work could cause one to return to his native state like the *Lord of the Flies*.

Drew found it odd that you could have such an itinerant counseling practice and that it could be conducted in public. Such an enterprise seemed like performing outpatient surgery on a park bench, but in his present circumstances he couldn't be very particular. He was careful to keep his voice down even if Clifford spoke at a robust volume, perhaps as a form of advertisement. The adjacent table was occupied by a woman in her late forties reading a book called *The Stranger Within*, which could have been anything from philosophy to horror. She also wore headphones, although Drew strongly suspected no sound was emitted and she was listening to their every word.

"How's the job hunt?" Clifford asked, getting down to business.

"When I mail a resume, I feel like I'm launching a message in a bottle across the Atlantic," Drew said, unable to temper his keen sense of frustration. "Nothing to report lately." A few days before, Drew had almost signed one of those plaintive letters, 'Yours truly, Osama Bin Laden,' in the hope they would at least notice the signature, but he kept that episode to himself.

"One of them is bound to pay off. It's just a numbers game."

Against his will, Drew remembered his last hour at Rimland, when his boss Perry Welker airbrushed the news of his imminent discharge with several strokes of Pollyannic nonsense. Welker had rattled on about how it wasn't drew's fault but merely a matter of "market forces," how the severance would tide him over so that whole affair would have the feel of an extended holiday.

"Anything else lately?" Cliff continued, in his unflappable manner.

"Nothing major. Well, there was one small thing."

Drew went on to recount an incident from that week when he'd practically been ejected from Nell's schoolyard. As he waited for her near the exit after her ballet class, a portly woman he'd never seen before emerged from behind a post and confronted him. "Excuse me, but you can't be here," she commanded. "You can't just loiter on this property—there's an ordinance against it."

Drew had the kind of face that somehow resembled others and this often led to confusion. He had been up late the night before and with her maternal alarms going off, the lady must have mistaken him for some derelict who had wandered over from the adjacent park. Did she imagine he'd just been jettisoned from the local shelter for the afternoon or that he had a shopping cart full of his worldly belongings hidden in the bushes? When he began to explain that he was waiting for his daughter, one of her friends from the neighborhood shouted, "It's okay, Mrs. Strickmeyer. That's Nellie's grandfather." It had further galled him to think Nell might have been teased because he was a bit older than the rest of the parents.

All in all, they had a fairly standard session, filled with Cliff's buoyant reassurances, his statistics on how losing one's career was at least as stressful as the death of a relative or having been mugged. He really shined in these diatribes which were as convincing as the Sermon on the Mount. He dispensed koans like "we have to keep the ball moving down the field" that were hopelessly broad and yet somehow appropriate to Drew's propensity for tangents. But if these maxims were the solution, why did he feel he was being diminished by the minute, the incredible shrinking Drew Runyon?

Drew had gotten so caught up in his avalanche of complaints that he was late getting home. In past years, one of the compromises Drew and Zoe had made to put money aside for retirement was having just one car, a 2007 Taurus, and it was her only means of getting all the way up north. In her agitation, Zoe heard him clomping up the flights of stairs, intercepting him even before he'd reached the landing, which was strewn with an assortment of boots, shovels, and ice-skates.

"I'm sorry," he huffed, still catching his breath. "I misjudged the time, but I'll drive you."

He understood how important it was to be prompt for an interview, how there was enough anxiety without factoring in the slickness and unpredictable delays. Through the hall window, they could both see the forecast snowstorm had arrived, its large flakes blanketing the yard.

"That would be nice, Drew. It would be one less thing to worry about."

She was dressed to make an irreproachable impression with a blazer over a skirt ensemble, and a compliment of makeup that never failed to transform her features in a way he never quite understood. He had counted on arrivng earlier with enough time to change into something more civilized, but that clearly wasn't the case. When they got to the car, he remembered warnings all over the news that some of the collision airbags were exploding like grenades.

"Why don't you sit there, honey? There's more room and it's safer." The fine snow was treacherous, and if he should skid into an otherwise innocuous fender bump, it would only be him who absorbed the impact of the balloon and any shrapnel that came with it.

"So it's the chauffer routine again?" On vacations, even before the alerts, they had often made this arrangement to keep Nell company as a diversion from all those miles of highway.

"Only if you want to."

"Yes, Jeeves," she said, shifting into a haughty accent. "Too bad the limo is in the shop, but this jalopy will have to do."

It occurred to Drew that the car did resemble a beaten-up taxi with its plain, oblong contour and a significant scratch over the left wheel casing. All it lacked was a checkered strip running around the chassis and a tented sign on the roof. Drew knew that Zoe sometimes liked to act as if she was somehow his superior, and the situation played right into this scenario, but he didn't want to stir things up and sabotage her prospects. It was all right for Zoe to occasionally disparage him because he knew beneath this was a bedrock of love.

"Where to ma'am?"

"I prefer 'miss.' 19 Prairie Plaza—I'm meeting a CEO for a million dollar deal."

"I hope you're a good tipper."

"Of course, that will depend on how comfortable the ride is," she said, relishing the game. "Sometimes I think you aim for the potholes."

He hadn't mentioned that Martin was one of the movers and shakers at the company because Zoe was one of those people who despised the notio of secret networks trumping merit. Of course, this was naive, a knd of unilateral disarmament, but he admired his wife's tenacity. Besides, Zoe really did seem perfect for the job as it was listed in the notice and he figured there couldn't be that much competition for a short term stint like that. Glancing over, he again marveled at how pretty she was when lost in thought, the salience of her lips and rich, umber eyes.

The interview was at the national headquarters in Westbrook, a fashionable suburb, seeded with private preserves and shot through with an inscrutable, winding pattern of streets. Its capricious system reminded Drew of the labyrinths of yore, meant to disorient any intruders who unwittingly drifted into them. Despite the circuitous route, they managed to arrive with ten minutes to spare, enough time for Zoe to compose herself and go over her lines, as if she had a part in a cheap production of summer stock.

Veering onto the long, sinuous drive that marked the property, Drew noted that it was flanked by medieval pennants hoisted on towering poles. The building was a six-story edifice, so abstract as to defy geometry, set back away from the street behind a stand of elm. He couldn't make up his mind if Zoe looked like she was about to be the subject of a coronation or of a firing squad. He gave her an encouraging pat on the shoulder as he dropped her off at the grand entrance.

"I'm afraid I've forgotten my pocketbook," she said, trying to ward off her tension. "You'll have to put it on my tab."

"Knock 'em dead," he replied, a little weary of the charade but genuinely wanting her to bowl the managers over.

"They're unlikely to give me the job if I did that." She was too keyed up to do anything but offer him a tight smile as he watched her make her way into the prisms of glass.

Drew almost got lost right from the first turn because all the angles were skewed and without any reference to the cardinal points. A GPS was out of the question, just another voice telling him what to do, but he made a mental note to buy a compass for the glove compartment. At least that way, when he got in the suburbs, he wouldn't find himself going in circles like a dazed Bedouin. He reversed course in a cul-de-sac, retraced his steps and went straight for a diner they'd gone by, the Ranch House, where he could sit with his book while Zoe was grilled on her life story.

He needed to kill some time, but his phone was a basic model that had no more ability to access the internet than a cigarette lighter. In his booth with a club sandwich and a Manhattan to salve his frayed nerves, he tried to read his book about the Trojan War. Still, Drew felt like an alien in this place decorated with saddles, steer horns, and fake cacti. He kept getting the Greeks and Spartans mixed up, so instead he thought about Langford, second guessing himself for not trying to pull that string.

He remembered a time at Tranmore as a gang from Delta Chi Epsilon watched a last-minute shot lift the basketball team into the conference finals. The image somehow captured the elation and camaraderie which seemed to define that stage of life. But the crassness of contacting Martin out of the blue for the favor would have been so transparent as to reduce their former acquaintance to a base transaction.

Such qualms hammered at Drew throughout his lunch, as he realized that they would have to collect Nellie from her dance class at four. Whenever one of her parents was not waiting when she emerged into the courtyard, she felt as if she'd been abandoned to a foster home, so he decided to head back a little early. Back in the visitors section, Drew left the car idling, so he could listen to a Blues disc. Waiting for Zoe's call, he became concerned he might damage the motor and shut it off.

The manner in which everything took longer than it should irked him; how long could it take to ascertain whether she could sketch a shelf or a serving tray? Drew had waited for things—laundry to dry, mechanics in filthy garages, cable repairmen and ticket agents—so often lately, that it had come to seem a kind of occupation. He spotted a frozen, man-made pond in a clearing behind the lot. Beside it, there was a flag with a corporate emblem, a castle complete with drawbridge and parapets. It had a welcome mat at the threshold, stamped with a smiling, crowned couple. Again he thought of Martin, warm inside his capacious quarters, probably with a panoramic view of the grounds.

Drew had always been curious about how the other half lived. As a kid, he'd jumped the fence at Hillcrest Country Club, trotted around the 18th green like a caddy, and peered into the opulent ballroom before he was forced to flee. But this time was different because for once he belonged; he knew someone inside. As with many executives, Martin might be in a Lear jet headed for some conference, avoiding winter in the midwest like the plague. But if he was there, Drew imagined Martin catching sight of him and being delighted that his long-lost classmate had stopped by after all these years.

The storm had passed, but the temperature was still nine degrees, and it didn't take long, with the heater off, before Drew was shivering. He noticed that his scarf, cashmere with a concentric design, the one decent article of clothing he'd worn that day, was missing. He quickly realized he had left it at the restaurant or the café, where it was likely to become part of someone else's wardrobe. And again he thought of Nell, how being late for a pickup on such a day simply wasn't an option. The snobs at Hamilton Elementary weren't going to get another reason to write him off.

The oppressive parking lot and its soulless rank of vehicles stood in utter contrast to the recessed glimmer of the citadel beyond them and Drew figured it couldn't really hurt if he lingered in the lobby for a few minutes. His very presence would suggest a certin timetable and might help to move things along. He was sure that his bulky anorak would conceal the dishevelment underneath.

Once sucked through the precisely curved revolving doors, the foyer was marvelously open, with a vaulted ceiling whose atrium deflected a ray of light, throwing its jagged edge to the far wall. In the center, there was a ring of brightly-colored lounges and sculpted tables in peculiar modern shapes. A small band of suited business types straddled a bank of elevators which was adorned by a fountain. Drew proceeded across the lush carpet that seemed to lend further buoyancy to the room and approached the imposing desk that formed a kind of checkpoint.

Drew waited at a certain distance while the receptionist engaged two clients in some procedural rite of passage. He kept thinking she would regard him but they kept talking and laughing quietly like they were in a library or a train car. He didn't want to give the impression of impatience—he hated how people sometimes hovered over fast-food cashiers as they frantically assembled their orders. So he retreated to the cluster of furniture with its seaside motif and canted chairs.

Next to the conditions outside, the interior had the cloying quality of a greenhouse. Having neglected to bring his book, Drew felt mortally unoccupied but spotted a spiral stand of brochures, plucked one out and began to absently flip through the pictures. He had to admit that the items it contained were all strangely pleasant in some insidious way and because he didn't want to be tempted, abruptly put the pamphlet down. He may have spun too fast because he immediately felt that familiar dizziness from the department stores, the sensation of being on a boat, where what lay beneath you was not solid.

Careful to hide his alarm as best he could, Drew wished Clifford would materialize with one of his silly aphorisms. But he needed to steady himself and lurched for a sort of couch, which had an unusual convex design. The back cushion was pushed at an obtuse angle almost like a recliner and when it didn't accept his leaning weight where he thought it would, he half tumbled off, barely catching himself with one hand.

Springing back up, Drew caught a flash of himself in a set of mirrors along an alcove. Those reflected the sweatshirt under his unzipped coat, which bore the much faded name of his distant alma mater, its purple lettering reduced to shadows. A lank of his wayward hair hung limply down his forehead from when he'd removed his pullover hat. Tamping it down, Drew became aware that back at the desk, the people had broken from their muted conversations and were now agape, barely masking their amusement. It was only then he noticed the set of velvet ropes on one side of the tableau and realized the furniture was just for display. The arranged merchandise formed a kind of exhibit, as illusory as the false dreams they were all peddling.

He glanced over to the sound of a woman's heels knocking along the polished oak floor. She moved briskly and with authority, like a guard in a female prison. Drew instinctively angled to cut her off before she rounded the counter, trying to seem casual, feigning the demeanor of a supplicant. She didn't stop as he gently approached, and he had the sense that she would hurl herself to the floor if he tried to get past her.

"Back again I see," she barked in a muffled tone. "I'm afraid you can't stay here. It's a place of business." If this wasn't enough, she wrinkled her nose, indicating the alcohol on his breath, and glared at him as if he were a reprobate who had just fallen off a barstool. "Whoever you're here for, I'll tell them the cab is waiting outside."

In his bewilderment, he nevertheless realized that a hidden camera must have captured him dropping Zoe off and recorded a piece of their exchange. There had undoubtedly been some complaint about the livery services.

"You don't understand. I'm just here for my wife. And I know the Vice-President. We were in the same club in college."

"Of course you were. And maybe if we can't find them, you'll have us search for the queen of England. Listen, I know it's cold outside, but this is a private compound and we must all abide by the rules."

Incredibly, this woman's voice seemed nearly a replica of the lady who had traduced him as he smoked a cigarette waiting for Nell to emerge in her ballet shoes. Drew was seized with the ludicrous desire to show her a photograph of his modest but very serviceable home on which they owed less than fifty grand, his plaques from the March of Dimes, his junior high cross-country medals, and the trophy he'd been awarded for the hole-in-one at Tomahawk Municipal. Drew could almost hear the precise notes of Clifford's admonition not to let fools get under his skin. But it was happening anyway, just as it had at Rimland before the final blow. His dignity was once again under assault and though he attempted to remember the importance of Zoe's mission, he had reached his limit.

"I have no intention of moving a fucking inch until my wife gets here," Drew said impassively.

Just as the woman reacted with a kind of bug-eyed, stricken disbelief and turned to get reinforcements, Drew heard a loud click on the level above him and glimpsed Langford rush out of his deluxe refuge and lean over the railing. At first, Drew could not tell whether his countenance betrayed any element of recognition. Martin stared for a good ten seconds, apparently trying to piece together what lay below him. He was slightly heavier than Drew recalled but still maintained the strong jaw and determined features he had always sported. The corporate logo looming behind him suggested the figure of an escutcheon. Drew summoned back Delta Chi's coat of arms, a Saxon shield with an eagle holding an arrow in its mouth, and the fraternity motto "Here always a refuge" appearing on a scroll.

Even in these circumstances, Drew felt the urge to call out their old cheer, as if they had just run into one another at an airport, but a strange paralysis had set in.

"Martin, it's Drew. Sorry about the disguise," he barely managed, but amid the odd acoustics of that cavernous foyer, his voice seemed frail and broken.

From his perch on the balcony, Martin squinted, fixing his eyes upon him like a powerful beam, yet from that height and perhaps seizing on the ragged outfit and graying hair, he still couldn't decipher the link. His expression became so derisive, it was evident he wouldn't recognize Drew even if he held up their yearbook. Suddenly it dawned on him the email Langford sent must have been of the generic variety, that he had probably forgotten to delete Drew's address among the dozens of others. Martin was wearing the exact same imperial, cross threaded suit as Welker had, and it was as if he held a key to the gilded inner chambers far from the peasants outside the gate. Drew supposed that once some privelege had been obtained, probably at great cost, it was a matter of defending that safe place, sawing off the ladders of those who would claim a piece of the treasure and pouring fiery ash over the ramparts to finish them off.

"I'm sorry but I'm in a meeting," he hoarsely shouted, signaling to the woman who had earlier threatened him. "You'll have to speak to Ms. Watkins," he added before vanishing into the seamless row of offices.

As if on cue, Zoe began to descend a zigzagging staircase, shepherded by another well dressed woman, who nodded and spoke in a steady stream. They both looked up for a moment to witness the tail end of the exchange and could not have failed to notice the awkwardness of it, nor the rigid bearing of Ms. Watkins. Yet they continued bantering like schoolgirls, so wrapped up in some personal anecdote that they ignored the charged atmosphere of the room. Drew heard the escort declare that they would be in touch soon as if the whole decision was a mere formality.

"There he is," Zoe said, gesturing vaguely, still making sure her pumps didn't catch the rug, but Drew was already sidling toward the exit. As she got closer, there was second where she seemed to recoil from the formless jumble of his coat and haphazard laces of his sneakers, but she quickly made her way to his side. A conclave had convened in a hallway that included uniformed men, arranged at the edge of the shielding glass.

"What did you do?" Zoe whispered, as the two of them whooshed through the impenetrable doors, out into the arctic air. Drew wouldn't have been able to say whether the notes in her question were born of annoyance, sorrow, shock, or disbelief but there seemed to be remnants of each. It had begun to snow again and a savage gust rose up to hurl the icy particles toward them. Drew met her puzzled stare, tried to silently soften the impact, convey that they would be all right, even without the approval of the fat cats, all the way to the end.

"I don't know but it doesn't matter. You're better than them. I couldn't bear to see you or Nell hurt by anything."

Zoe sagged a little and began to say something but she knew there were no words for these collisions of the heart and that they would have to hurry to reach their daughter in time. Reluctantly, she allowed Drew to slip his arm around hers and tug her close so that that they moved in tandem, bracing themselves against the chill beyond the concourse. They did not look back at the imposing structure or their reflections briefly wavering across the front of it. The security detail probably figured that closer pursuit might just inflame the situation, and kept vigil from inside. The Runyons were doing what the company wanted anyway, leaving the premises forever.

## *Satellite View*

From our kitchen alcove, I could see Mariel Crane kneeling in her garden and even hear her humming some tune, the name of which seemed just over the borderline of memory and would probably remain there. The Cranes' three dogs, two Irish setters and a collie, were not with her. Perhaps they would be too much of a distraction, with all the barking and chasing over the Adirondack chairs and around the trampoline. It was pleasant to watch her from that height as she stretched and worked the ground, the back of her baggy jeans twisted, a thick brown braid curled along her neck, as her hands sought out some offending weed. This was Saturday morning, probably my favorite time of the week; its quiet lack of urgency enhanced by oblique light, the steam from a mug of coffee and the purr of a hedge trimmer somewhere down the block. I could not help myself and glanced up again to see Mariel wipe her hands on the sides of her admirably lean torso. But I broke off as soon as the fascination with spying began to exert itself, as I didn't want to get drawn in too far.

We had only exchanged a few words over the oak paneled fence, perhaps because Corrie and I had no space in the back except a narrow path to the dumpster. It was as if we were situated on different levels, which interfered, like an atmospheric imbalance, with normal communication. It was more common for a trace of their sumptuous cooking, that purgatorial scent of bacon or barbecued chicken with a hint of lighter fluid to waft across the property line, and strike with the vigor of an aphrodisiac. Their garden was impressive. They grew giant chrysanthemums and violets, and a strain of sunflowers so large as to seem predatory.

Mariel had a part-time job selling cosmetics and practiced Tai Chi in the early mornings. I had only witnessed the latter once, but the slowness of her movements, in some long formless shift, exerted a magnetic pull hardly less than the gravity of Jupiter. I knew this desire for her was just a shallow function of the unknown, a mirage of the senses, and that Corrie's absence was propelling me back to some cavalier feeling from bachelor days. Corrie was just as beautiful, with her dark eyes and slender calves, but it was a beauty fraught with trouble. A rattling timer went off inside the Cranes' house, and, without even discarding her gloves, Mariel jogged back inside the porch where she remained safe from any further surveillance.

Corrie had flown to a resort in Antigua for ten days with her friends, Sarah and Diane, compliments of a special package Sarah won in a raffle. In six years, Corrie and I had never vacationed separately, but there was only the one ticket, and Corrie seemed at a stage whereby some connubial distance might be a tonic. Under different circumstances, I might have welcomed a few days apart to diffuse the ineffable sameness that can envelop a marriage, but her departure seemed yet another variable in a delicate equation.

Sometime in May, I had a check for the mortgage bounce and when I asked Corrie about it, she confessed she'd gone into an off-track betting parlor after running an errand downtown. She had always loved animals and decided that she needed a margarita. Then, she became intrigued by the races that were shown on several TV's all over the room—the look of the scoreboard, the rapt attention, and the crescendo of the rooting at the screens. The palm trees in the background reminded her of her island home. She read the names of the horses on the program: "Scarlet Mood," "Strange Rhythm," "Jamaica Starlight," and so on. It got her thinking about the origin of those names and one thing led to another.

She said that her horse placed in the first race and she went through $440 from the ATM machine by the end of the afternoon. Of course, she didn't like losing the money, but the smooth umber track and fluid movement of the thoroughbreds seemed to banish the Midwestern ice and gloom for a few hours. After that pleasant interlude, she had surreptitiously been going back every other week.

I wondered what her friends on the trip would say to her if she made some plea to divert their course to a racetrack or a waterside casino. Despite her assurances, I continued to have the sense that nearly any of our most cherished possessions could disappear with no more cause than a misguided hunch, some utterly baseless intuition. I knew Sarah and Diane might exert some subtle, almost tidal influence, but you never knew with women on a jaunt. They might all be out drinking a pitcher of daiquiris and betting the farm.

The phone rang, its shrill notes bursting into my thoughts like an air raid.

"We're on the ground, Gavin," Corrie said, with some billowy flutter in the background. "It's hot but wonderful. I can't wait to get to the ocean."

"That's great sweetheart. Did you get much turbulence?"

"Not that I know of. I slept half the way . . . . Did you go out last night?"

"Just to Harrigan's for dinner. I stayed for a couple drinks and read my book at the bar."

"Did people look at you strangely?"

"You know they did. It's practically taboo. You'd think I was making a bomb . . . ."

It occurred to me to seek something in her voice; a tremor, a hesitance, some off note, which might signal our bank account was about to be drained. But she was unreadable even under normal circumstances, and the line made her sound like she was in an underground cavern.

"Have you run out of battery from all the photographs yet?" I said, a familiar joke.

Before the family embezzlement was revealed, Corrie had persuaded me of the necessity of a video camera. Despite my general aversion to pictures, it had been fun for the first few days, seeing her delight in the images she recorded at the park or the arboretum. But by the third weekend, she seemed to be turning our life into a documentary. She would film the mailman sauntering from the curb and cars routinely ignoring the stop sign at the end of the block. The last straw was when I woke to her filming me just as I broke into the haze of consciousness with matted hair, a rancid taste in my mouth, and crust in my eyes. I threatened to fling the contraption in the lake and watch it sink, with all its potential for needless preservation down to the murky, algae-filled bottom.

"Not quite. I didn't think it was a good idea to take the camera on the plane. They might have gotten the wrong idea and hustled me off to Guantanamo."

"Do you have an itinerary or are you just going to play it by ear?"

"You know Diane and Sarah. They're free spirits. I guess we'll just go where the wind blows us."

I was determined not to give the impression that I didn't trust her, anything which would make her even more impelled to recklessness. I suspected it was something about me that had driven her to gamble. Unlike a lot of people, I possess the capacity to trace any evil, no matter how remote, back to some comment or act of negligence on my part. In a certain humor, I could be convinced I had turned a wrong valve and initiated a roundabout chain of events that caused the icecaps to melt. But my forbearance was mostly due to an old indiscretion of my own. Several summers before, I had made a large investment—in a combined golf and archery range—without Corrie's knowledge. The entire sum had gone up in smoke when the city council threw the consortium a curve, and the whole episode remained as hidden as Blackbeard's treasure.

"Just be careful not to wander into the bad areas at night," I almost yelled to overcome the clamor of street merchants besieging her. "And have a good time . . . that's the main thing."

The other women returned from their expedition, and Corrie laughed at some remarks they made that I didn't catch. "Everyone's boarding the bus, Gavin," she shouted, in a hail of static and other sounds that might have been from the jostling of a queue. "Don't be staying up too late."

With Herculean restraint, I managed not to mention the casinos, and only heard, "Oh shoot . . . ." and then nothing. Amid the surge of vendors, the fragile connection had been snatched away.

The next morning when it seemed most everyone had fled to church, our cat Falstaff escaped through a crack in the screen door. He apparently discovered a breach in the Cranes' privet, wriggling into their yard. I didn't realize it until I happened to see him sniffing around the badminton net. To call a cat from some forbidden adventure is like imploring the sky for rain, but for a minute I did so anyway. My desperate tone only seemed to intensify his feline contempt. Despite my general reticence about invading someone's privacy, I rushed down the steps, catching an ankle at the landing, and limped over to the Cranes' front door.

The bell was in the shape of a squash racquet, and I nervously jabbed at it. This imposition was the kind of unwanted disturbance phone hustlers were always causing me, and for a second I anticipated the annoyed stare I had encountered canvassing for an environmental group one summer in college. No one answered the door after several rings, which carried the timbre of a dentist's drill. I almost peeked inside but wondered if I might not catch Mariel in a sheer kimono and cause her to scream. There was no stirring behind the opaque curtains, and when I went around the house, via the gangway, the gate was unlocked. Pushing through, I had merely a more intimate vantage of the scene I had observed a thousand times.

There again was the huge sign of Hoffenbrau, with its heraldic icon—a fierce looking lion with wings and talons. There was the tool shed and the trampoline with its fading orange fabric and the small stone patio. Falstaff's location was not at first apparent, but I was so captive to the novelty of my position, with a sense of giddiness almost, that the reason for my being there was momentarily suspended. Then, as I spotted him nosing around the grill, and catching a glimpse of me, he darted through a crevice in the side of the garage. I walked over with a nonchalant stride, as if there were a party in progress, pushed the rotten door open enough to squeeze through, and grabbed for him with a swift and vengeful motion. But I was no match for Falstaff's olympian reflexes, and the animal darted between a surfboard and a broken grandfather's clock.

It was no secret that the Crane's garage was stuffed to the ceiling with the remnants of a hundred rummage sales. Apparently, Lou liked to collect old furnishings and bric-a-brac simply for the sake of doing so. He had pillows in the shapes of elephants, archaic board games whose rules had been lost to history, umbrella racks, seafaring trunks, coiled carpets, volumes of books whose pages were as brittle as papyrus, and a harp. Whether this penchant for worthless accumulation might be explained by some childhood trauma or neurotic proclivity was far from clear. In any case, the room pressed in upon me like the aftermath of an implosion.

I found an inconspicuous corridor winding through the ruin, which led not only to our cat but to a cache of erotica that rivaled the back room of a well-stocked porn shop. There were statues in explicit positions, hundreds of filthy magazines, paraphernalia for sex the use of which I could only speculate on. This was Lou's dirty little hoard, and no doubt the rest of the heap was mere camouflage. If Mariel were to find out, would she recoil from him as from some weird, lurking stranger? And might she accept comfort from a sympathetic neighbor should my own marriage also be dashed in a slot machine? I gathered up Falstaff, where he had alighted on a painting of nymphs being pursued by a lurid satyr, and got off the premises as quickly as I could. When I did, I was relieved to see the tranquil morning shade and Rob Jarmon obliviously trying to start his lawnmower.

After work on Monday, the flat felt eerily vacant, so I decided to walk to the lake. This was something I often did when the weather cooperated, stroll around those rarified precincts near the beach, scrutinizing the homes of the gentry. I could let my mind wander, crossing through alleys, observing the intricate details of increasingly affluent homes as I made my way toward the shore. Even though the sun would be sinking on the opposite side and blocked as it set, the feel of the sand, the serene currents, the chameleon changes of color on the surface as the light faded from turquoise to some deeper shade, the vacant life guard outposts, the buoys and catamarans all helped sooth the frictions of the day.

My sunset tours always took a certain route, and over the years I had observed a number of the backyards' distinctive features. There was a putting green in one yard complete with a flagstick in the hole, the grass hewn to such a fine degree it could have been a Persian rug. Inside another, a birdbath flanked by cherubs caught in a perpetual frolic had a jagged shard of stone missing, as if it had been there for centuries. The surrounding bushes were trimmed with such a fine geometry that they looked as solid as furniture. A giant satellite dish facing south fixed on an invisible object making the same imperceptible revolutions as the earth, peering down from its smooth, floating orbit.

The place that belonged to Warren and Joyce Beaumont, their names inscribed on a small plaque near the castle-like entrance, seemed to hold a particular intrigue. It had clean, simple lines, and the powerboat hitched to a trailer in the driveway lent it a kind of insouciance. Peering between the slats of the perfectly symmetric stockade fence, I saw a broad lawn with a massive sugar maple, its limbs and foliage yawning east and west. A precisely arranged pile of chopped wood and a playground set led up to a treehouse that looked as if it might have been designed by Frank Lloyd Wright.

The house was utterly still, with no sign of electrified alarm systems. I felt emboldened to find the latch on the gate and was amazed when it fell open, as tempting as a skirt riding up a pair of smoky, slender thighs. It was so much easier this time just to follow the allure of curiosity, as if summoned by a siren song, and I felt that old burglar's rush of forbidden entry.

The light in that space was sublimely soft, making amorphous patterns, which oscillated in the breeze. The back porch and adjacent yards carried the unnatural quiet of desertion, as if the occupants had all fled to their cottages. There was a miniature gazebo, Chinese lanterns with indecipherable characters etched on the sides, a latticed railing on the portico, and an arbor, which afforded the spot a monastic calm. I saw that the play area had the usual fortress motif with climbing bars and a twisting circular slide angled to the ground. The treehouse rose up from a century old black walnut and seemed a perch from which the whole neighborhood could be scanned.

The two quick shots of bourbon I'd gulped before leaving the house, no doubt, aided my climb to the lofted platform. I was still athletic enough to negotiate the footholds, and except for an instant of vertigo, I made the last lunge through the small opening of the structure with relative ease. There was more room than one might have imagined from the outside, and the windows made me think of the portals of a ship. From there, I could see over all the barriers that divided the sections of land, and one angle even offered a sliver of the lake containing a lone sail. One could still make out whorls in the boards like a cluster of ingrained eyes. The roost seemed vestigial, the children for whom it had been so lovingly constructed having grown up and moved away.

It seemed clear that the Beaumonts had several houses stationed around the country, in which to settle for established seasons. I visited the treehouse a few times when there were no lights in the house and gradually came to have a squatter's sense of belonging. The first few times I stole away there, I was careful not to leave evidence of my intrusion. But as the days passed without any hint of movement near the immense building, I relaxed, and the hideout took on the aspect of a private sanctuary.

At various times, I brought a candle, binoculars, a pack of Macanudo cigars, a biography of Churchill, and a lithograph of Carmel Bay. I could usually attain a comfortable position in the main compartment by leaning against one of the beams. As dusk came in tiny degrees, I simply sat, surveying that small piece of the neighborhood and wondered at the strange necessity of secret lives. Might there be an envelope of Mariel's own nude photographs in Lou's stash, taken to preserve her physical zenith for posterity? Was Corrie's gambling habit merely one of a nearly limitless array of deceits and veiled compulsions, so that the real core of her was as unknown to me as the bizarre markings on an ancient tablet?

The next day Corrie called and left a message that they were having a wild time and headed to someplace called the Driftwood Inn. I wondered if she sounded a bit drunk or this slurring of vowels was merely the effect of interference. There was the brief zing of what might be the start of a peptic ulcer, and it was not hard to imagine our leather couch and drafting table being unceremoniously carted into a waiting van.

The following night I had just passed beneath the viaduct when the cell phone rang with its strange metallic version of the first few measures of "Rhapsody in Blue." The receiver immediately contained evidence of commotion: bells, shouts, perhaps the rush of some vehicle or the breaking of a wave.

"Hello sweetheart. It doesn't sound like you," Corrie said.

"Hi Corrie. Who do I sound like?"

"I'm not sure exactly . . . . Some other version of you."

"What have you been doing out there? Have you gone native yet?"

"Yes, the locals have us in papaya skin dresses and worship us as goddesses of the moon."

"Just so long as they don't start making any sacrifices. You should discourage that."

"We'll try."

"How are Diane and Sarah?"

"They're like bloodhounds. They barely let me out of their sight."

I wondered about that supervision for a second, whether it represented a positive or negative development. We talked for a while about nothing in particular; about how I'd forgotten my password at work again, about how she'd had swordfish for dinner. There was no hint in her tone that might betray a torrid rendezvous on some playboy's yacht or the purchase of a rare emerald.

"I have to go, Gavin, because we're beginning to break up. Must be the atmosphere or something."

I imagined that she suddenly had to get off the phone to mask her grief that Zanzibar, a longshot she couldn't resist, had just fallen to the back of the pack, putting her five grand in the red.

"Never say that, Corrie. That we're beginning to break up. It's bad luck."

"What?"

"Nothing"

"See you in a couple days," she said, with what seemed like wistfulness but could have been a hundred other things.

That evening in the treehouse, I fumbled through the theatre section of the *Times* with a flask of Crown Royal set on a crude shelf. It suddenly occurred to me that I hadn't seen Mariel Crane in her arbor for a week, that my best opportunity for the kind of casual exchange, which might lead to something more had come and gone. I was exhausted, and the shadows of the candle against the grainy wood must have been playing tricks in the twilight because her elegant image coalesced out of the cocoon of leaves beyond the nearest branch and hovered in the air. She wore a diaphanous, lavender gown that only accentuated the salient contours of her body. She moved straight toward me with her hand extended, but it was unclear if she were asking me to dance or making an urgent plea for rescue. I sat rapt with the certainty that once she reached me, we were bound to seize one another in a feral embrace, the inexorable product of some long suppressed hunger. I knew I would be as powerless to resist her at that moment as Corrie would be captive to raiding every cent in our nest egg for the chance to live another life, a more exalted life, even for a little while.

While I groped for my bearings, the apparition quickly dissolved as the mansion's owners unceremoniously came out onto the porch. They looked to be in their late forties, which appeared to confirm my theory of the fort's abandonment. They had decided to dine *al fresco,* and, though their faces were indistinct, I could see they had a bottle of wine and what looked like a leg of lamb. For a while, they did not talk, and there was only the abrasive sound of silverware clinking against plates. When they finally spoke, I could only catch a few words here and there and had to suppose the rest like a puzzle.

I had not bargained on my hideaway being a vehicle for eavesdropping, but unconsciously I started leaning closer, praying that the whole structure wouldn't shift or cause me to lose my balance and plummet onto the jungle gym. Their meal seemed to be suffused with tender apologies, over some incident that had rocked them, *mea culpas* issuing back and forth. The only full sentence I heard was when the man said, "You know it's been a long while since that time in the gazebo." For a minute, they were silent, and then they arose and abruptly went inside. Though perfectly within their rights, it seemed unfair to close me off at that crucial juncture. It was as if the last play of a tied game had been preempted by the five o'clock news.

I tried to resume contact with Mariel, but the spell had been broken and there was no trace of her, except I could have sworn that the subtlest current of some unfamiliar cologne drifted along the ceiling. The lights along the cul-de-sac flicked on, as if to expose me. Then the couple emerged, arm in arm, the woman in a different funneling dress. The gazebo had a swinging bench in it and was only a few feet from the branches where I was concealed. It seemed that they meant to engage in some kind of lovemaking and to spy in such a situation seemed to put me in the same league of hedonism as Lou Crane. I had no other choice than to make a quick retreat while they made their way out onto the flagstones.

It was very dark by that point, with only a scythe of a moon low on the horizon and the wan light from the street and surrounding house windows. I capped my bottle and hurried down, but in my anxiety slipped on the curve of the tube slide, which generated a loud, hollow report.

"What was that?" Mrs. Beaumont said, with more than a hint of agitation . . . . "Are the raccoons back?"

"Who's there?" Warren demanded, with that particular indignation of the wealthy. "Go inside Joyce. I'll get the flashlight."

"Just call 911, Warren. Please don't try to be a hero."

Once on the ground, where my ankle throbbed from the awkward jump, my usual egress seemed too far, and I vaulted over the lower fence into the adjacent yard. I landed in a patch of hydrangeas and crouched below the hazy flicker of a TV in the recesses of the occupant's family room. Again, there seemed no avenue of escape by the front way, so I scaled the cabin cruiser and leapt into the alley. As Warren warily descended the steps, I could see the signature beam of a flashlight, its small radius of illumination erratically darting across the trees, and I thought that the way Warren bore his other arm, he might be carrying a gun.

"For God's sake Warren, let the police handle it," Joyce said,with a hush of mounting urgency.

I ran as fast as I had since my cross-country days in high school until I reached the sidewalk, where I turned the corner and affected the gait of someone on a stroll. I pulled out my phone and pretended to be trapped in some moronic exchange that I've seen people have while walking their

Labradors or ransacking the aisles of a supermarket. My voice seemed natural, despite the fact that no one was hearing it at some remote location, and I paused at various intervals, listening to the other end of the phantom dialogue.

It was not until I reached the main thoroughfare, a couple blocks away with its reassuring twenty-four hour grocery store, Thai restaurant, and car dealership that I heard the siren and then saw frenetic bursts of light on the police car that zoomed past. Would they inspect the cigar butt I had left for fingerprints, swab it for DNA? Had my tennis shoes left a characteristic imprint of squiggled lines? I imagined a scenario where Lou Crane was revealed as an outrageous collector of smut while I was charged with criminal trespass and branded a peeping Tom. Two minutes later, I was home washing the dirt off my shoes in the bathtub like a hardened fugitive.

Corrie returned the next day in a cab from the airport, which had already dropped off her companions. "Hello honey!" she cried. "I thought you might have been on one of your walks."

"I just didn't feel like it tonight. How was it?"

"It was great but I'm exhausted. I feel like I've been to the ends of the earth."

I paid the driver and embraced her awkwardly before the door was even closed. Through her almost narcotic fatigue, she seemed genuinely happy to see me, but this enthusiasm could have been merely the effect of guilt at having lost a fortune at the roulette wheel or the strange gentleness that often precedes an irrevocable split.

While I struggled to balance her bags, she described some ritual they performed in the village where people were just hurling themselves around like they were in a trance. The Cranes pulled into their driveway just then, apparently returning from a camping trip. Lou was occupied carrying the posts and canvas of an enormous tent large enough to shelter a half dozen of some roaming tribe. I could find nothing lascivious or depraved in the way he struggled moving across the patio. Mariel trailed behind, looking thoroughly ordinary in some unflattering shorts, as she kept the dogs at bay. Her perfunctory glance and wave did not seem the gestures of someone concealing the tempests of an illicit passion.

"It's funny how when you come back from someplace everything looks different," Corrie said. "Do I really live here?"

This was enough to cause my heart to speed full throttle and brace for some tale of imminent bankruptcy or divorce. Had she experienced some epiphany that made her former life unbearable? But then, she nearly collapsed in laughter when Falstaff got stuck climbing the screen door to see her, burying her neck in my shoulder, as I staggered along the porch.

"Until Falstaff evicts us," I said.

A week later, with the sun falling a fraction slower, even from a distance, I could tell that the treehouse had been taken down, and I experienced a visceral shock at its absence. For a moment, I simply could not imagine the refuge, which had supported me so comfortably, had been dismantled. Not even a hint remained, and the maple now seemed somehow naked and unprotected. There rose a tremendous impulse to dash over the hedge and through the obstacle course of lots stitched together on and on all the way to the lake's edge, to find another improbable place, like the mind's eye itself, from which to see without being seen. I never mentioned the Cranes' garage or the treehouse to Corrie for the same reason you never brought up some brief, sordid affair you once had, which vanished like some elusive object in the night sky. It was something that had been real once but no longer was, as if it had never happened at all.

## *A Stranger in Transit*

Oh, how I miss that announcement on the Metra Line, the sweet litany of stations stretching north along the shore. The list now seemed like the line-up for a great and vanished baseball team or a chant of Hindu deities: Clybourn, Ravenswood, Rogers Park, Wilmette, Indian Hill, Winnetka, Glencoe, Hubbard Woods, Braeside, Lake Forest, Lake Bluff, Winthrop Harbor . . . . The commute had always been a kind of fleeting respite where one could study a face, stare vacantly at the nuances of an intersection or a cemetery—a pleasantly repetitive limbo. The sound of each stop conjured its own image of commerce or the refuge of yards, viewed from above the trestle's gentle grade. That's why the judge's sentence banning me from my local route at Braeside for two years is so acutely painful. There are days when it feels as if I have been deported and become an exile, yet without the benefit of being physically removed, whereby you could lose yourself in the anonymous currents of some ruined city.

Now, after a rushed, ill-tempered twenty-minute drive full of pointless holdups, I am relegated to the caprice and jostle of the elevated train, the so called express, which is no more express than a movie line that winds around the block. It is fitted with austere plastic seats, and you are routinely jolted across metal bars and twisted by leather straps, provided to keep passengers from being flung into one another. The hues on the El are garish, and the ceiling is ringed with oblong ads for bankruptcy advice and miracle elixirs. The cars seem hollow and insubstantial as they waver, angling around a curve like a cheap amusement park ride. From Wilmette, they run parallel to the rails of my old shuttle, so that at some points, I am able to peer across through those opaque windows, to the placid contentment of my former life, before diverging through a dense and blighted corridor.

When those other tracks are visible, how can I not strain for a glimpse of Magdelena, whose soft curls on my neck are so inextricably woven with my banishment? She has not surfaced again, though I have haunted the platforms at certain times, panned the corners and surrounding shops for some semblance of her walk, her gentle shape. It is like searching for the light of an engine in the distance, but I cannot help but believe she will reappear, as if out of a mist one evening, and allow me to tell my version. Sometimes that's all one needs is to tell his side of the story, in the shadow land between conviction and repentance. Let me remember it for the hundredth time, not that the whole business can be changed one iota, but allow me to do that much.

That morning began as banal and exasperating as any other. I remember running for the train, vaulting two steps at a time like some slow-motion hurdler, and just reaching the coach in time, as the last of the waiting cluster sullenly boarded. But the doors closed on my briefcase, and I had to yank it free, as if from a set of jaws, before heading into the compartment. On the way downtown, we passed a stationary freight so close, the somber boxcars blotted out the nascent sun, casting us all in deep shade. It was the dead of winter, a January morning with all its bleak implications. Some scattered snow was being driven in a slanted descent, battering whatever lay in its path.

The familiar scenes scuttled by with the smell of diesel, the pulsing drone of the engine and the occasional squeal of the breaks in the background. You pass through a residential section whose far border marks a retail district and then an industrial zone, with its forlorn tableaus of abandoned machinery, dank outbuildings, rusting bay doors and piles of stone. Thick white smoke pouring from chimneys remained in tight, slow-drifting lines before dispersing, due to some property of the cold. It was suspended at a threshold of gravity, too heavy to rise and yet too weightless to fall. Small statues beckoned from the roof of a factory facing the tracks: a gargoyle, a nude, a bust of an Indian extending a peace pipe, a cherub. Grain elevators were staggered in a column like missile silos. Farther along the route, there was a place where the tracks crossed and merged, giant pieces of equipment sprawled at the edge, unreal almost in their discarded repose.

As my career was in advertising, I always noticed the stuff of our trade marring the landscape. There was the painted sign on the back of a warehouse announcing 1-800-good dog: THE LOVING METHOD THAT WORKS. Another, drawn on the brick facade of a grocery, showed a disembodied hand shaking its counterpart, over the phrase "Making Friends Through Conversation." Not far from the terminal, on the pitched side of a roof, as if were being beamed into space, there was a girl with an umbrella shielding herself from a shower of salt under an enormous caption, "When It Rains It Pours." I have no idea what such images mean except that these sights were part of my destiny, the current of my days.

I was sitting in one of my usual spots, on the East side where light would come in, with a vantage of an exit. There were times where I would attempt to look vaguely sick and even mildly deranged so that other passengers would veer away, but this occasion was not one of them. The snow seemed to let up, while I scanned the *Tribune* for some item of interest. We halted at the Ravenswood station, with its backdrop of a bank, a diner and, on the other side, a column of bungalows.

At first, the woman was there only peripherally, and I was abiding by the code that one should not acknowledge a stranger in transit who had by mere circumstance been thrust next to you. But the pressure on the cushion beneath us had been subtle, and the scent of jasmine was evocative, such that I could not help but raise myself up a little. Somehow I knew that at the rim of my ambient vision sat a beauty the likes of which I had never been so close to before.

Not wanting to frighten her off, I sipped my coffee from its styrofoam cup and feigned oblivion. I made no movement at all to betray that I even noticed her presence, except to pull in my elbows and allow her more room to read her paperback. She removed it from a small travel bag in a quiet, economical way. With an imperceptible glance, I could make out the title—*Mr. Murder*. I had never read a single mystery in my life, but suddenly the genre seemed imbued with some ineffable charm. As we sat with an almost unnatural stillness among the murmuring, sleepy crowd, I tried to restrain myself from the kind of furtive peeks, which must annoy anyone who has ever been jammed into a common space.

No one was more aware that these early-morning rituals are sacrosanct, and there's nothing worse than some boor on the make who violates them. Yet amid the usual crush of bulky overcoats and bags and laptop computers, the bumps and curves of the ride, I couldn't resist the occasional oblique view: the lovely, not too pronounced arc of her calves, the calm expectancy of her eyes. In that millisecond, I could also gather that she wore a long wool skirt, sleek boots, a high-necked lavender blouse. Her skin was perfect like a windswept dune, a single strand of gold encircling her neck. There was some serene cast to her features, a hint of Asian provenance.

To be honest, I was almost content with this proximity to her, as if I were seated at the table of a magnificent starlet and didn't want to ruin it with some obnoxious, fawning exhibition. I had not come close to sleeping with a woman since my divorce proceeding sixteen months before, and since then had been moving through the world with the tentativeness of someone who had been burned in an electrical fire. As we clattered toward the loop, I was merely going to read the paper and enjoy the palpable charge of her proximity. But then, as I tried to focus on a story about a fight to save a landmark kiosk from the wreckers' ball, her book was suddenly resting against her purse and her head, with its cataracts of dark, swirling hair was beginning to tilt, to fall. She pulled it upright once or twice, but then it was on the back of the seat and in about half a minute, in a dreamlike sequence, it came to rest on my shoulder.

Somehow I managed to pretend that this action was a commonplace event, that I was accustomed to the insomnia that could impel anyone to doze off amid the monotonous rocking of a train. Out the window, another freight brought a new round of companies on the sides of the cars: Cotton Belt, Pacific Northern, Golden West, Sandersville, Canadian National, Gondola Connection, Overland. The names alone comprised a siren song of sweet distance, a kind of lullaby. I suppose I could have shifted to gently awaken her but could not bring myself to do it.

The conductor, a man named Hennessey, who I'd come to regard as hopelessly disgruntled in his employment, came around to review our tickets. He went hurriedly down the rows, probably behind schedule, with his usual look of suspicion. He would sometimes abandon a transaction and half jog to pull the lever that separated the doors, with their faint hydraulic whir. One could see that he feared bumping into an elbow and sending the contents of a cup across an entire section. The effect was of one of those horses at the harness track, doomed never to break stride.

For a few minutes, the woman slept there as insouciant as a child while I merely attempted to remain inert, just let her get the rest she must have so desperately needed. The hem of her skirt slid precariously across her almost unbearably lovely knees with the light jouncing of the tracks. As the towering downtown edifices came into view, she stirred without any startled movement, as naturally as she might have in a five-star hotel. I permitted myself a brief sidelong look and hoped with all my being that she wouldn't misinterpret the situation and scream. After all, I had not drugged her or made her the subject of some nefarious plot, but in her confusion perhaps she would not know this.

"Oh, I'm sorry," she managed to say, her face acquiring a certain rosiness, as she disengaged herself and pulled slowly to the other side. "And it's only Tuesday. How am I going to manage the rest of the week." She turned her neck a couple times from side to side to release the tension.

"I understand. Used to happen to my aunt . . . . She once fell asleep in the 8th row of a boxing match."

"It's never happened before. I took a sleeping pill last night and . . . ."

"I know. Some of that stuff could tranquilize an elephant," I said, for no other reason except that I was dizzy with her countenance, and I could think of nothing else. She only regarded me with a benign yet quizzical expression, reminding me of some incredible actress like Jessica Alba or Frida Pinto. We had arrived at the terminal, and she pulled herself groggily up into the aisle but then turned around.

"I suppose we've met somehow. My name's Magdelena." Revealing this part of her, she issued an uneasy but still alluring smile, the sort that can linger in memory a long time. I had all I could do to carry out my side of the introduction and with the most hesitant meeting of our eyes, she was gone.

Though I held out little hope of any subsequent liaison, in the week that followed, I wore my best ties and scrutinized every inch of the Ravenswood station when we briefly came to a halt there. I tried the 7:21 and the 7:56, but she was like some phantom, which had risen from the depths of romantic despair. In my own town one evening, I rounded the corner and for a moment thought I glimpsed Magdelena's profile and some aspect of the jacket she had been wearing that day, the beige collar or pattern of buttons, but this resemblance turned out to be some other woman being dragged down the block by her Cocker Spaniel. Then, I was immediately petitioned by one of the beggars who spring from the halfway house in my neighborhood. They congregate in the small park across the street, passing the time with strange talk, aimless wandering, and vacant stares. He said, "Excuse me, sir, but I'm a descendent of Welsh Kings but have fallen on hard times. Could you give me five dollars for something to eat?" Handing over a pile of accumulated change, I said, "a royal line?" and he didn't retract an inch. "Oh yes, but you know how families are." For some reason, this seemed to deflate my hopes of ever finding Magdelena again, and I resolved to put her out of my mind lest I wind up in some desolate gangway murmuring her name.

I continued to slog through the series of small, lacerative aggravations, which were the hallmark of my existence. In an Italian café on the way to work, I spent ten minutes behind a heavyset woman while she languidly gathered napkins and stirred multiple bags of sugar into her coffee, as if she were setting up camp. At the bottleneck of the lone bridge, a frenzied commuter with a golf umbrella the circumference of a nomad's tent almost put my eye out with one of its spokes. Later that week, a man in a frayed stocking cap held the newspaper box open and asked if I wanted one, effectively offering to facilitate petty larceny. When I declined, he seemed rebuffed and stalked off muttering a string of curses.

At work, I tripped over an arching plant, which had been installed under a skylight to bring the ambiance up a notch, wrenching my heel and bend-ing a couple branches permanently across a vent. I had been trapped on a project with a colleague for five months. He had slick hair and was such a captive of cigarettes that he wore a trail in the carpet through the lobby where he was forced to stand outside in any weather. He had inherited a large house in Mexico and always seemed to have a cold from being shut up in the plane going back and forth. He was the sort of guy who would stand too close and engage you in some debate about the Middle Ages or welfare reform, even if you were carrying a refrigerator.

I would get a missive from my ex-wife Libby once in a while, perhaps out of guilt or maybe the sense that some vestigial feeling of our six years together might be redeemed. We would have a civil, if remote exchange of basic information, yet in the end, such contact never failed to dredge up the rancor of our breakup. Somewhere along the line, I had found that I could nearly discern her heart but always there was a threshold of mystery, a point beyond which one could not go. When she finally left for Pennsylvania, her parting words had been, "I hope you find somebody, David, but if you don't change I might be the last one—the end of the line."

On the train, faded baseball diamonds and warehouses and ads for cruises and pharmacies and tires continued to float by along the route. Trying not to think of Magdelena, I noticed the various designs of the shoes that were canted on the upper railing of the double deck and how those passengers had to crouch while they eased their way down the narrow steps. I observed there was almost no personal business people would not perform during their passage. They will sort their mail, apply mascara directed by tiny mirrors, cut out articles from a magazine, and have an intimate phone conversation everyone in range could recite word for word.

Over the years, I had seen so many people in various attitudes of travel, I would get the odd sensation of being able to read their thoughts. The old gentleman in the front seemed to reminisce about some escapade with a chorus girl in her dressing room. The tycoon in pinstripes was rehearsing the opening lines of some crucial speech. A black lady with a large package appeared to sway remembering some hymn that had swept her up since she was a girl. It was like the clairvoyance of the billboards, which at times seemed to reach right into the essence of my private condition and suggest some hidden core of understanding.

The only real flaw in my idyllic forty-five minute sojourn was Hennessey. My daily antagonism with him had resumed with all its unspoken vehemence. I was not one to buy a monthly ticket with its implications of privileged membership. I suppose this reluctance was also due to my having once lost a monthly the day after its purchase, which felt like igniting a pile of twenty-dollar bills. The ten-ride tickets had to be punched, which took more time for the conductors, and besides I never placed them in the metal holders for fear that in my foggy distraction I would leave them behind. I had barely avoided a skirmish with him that morning when a short man wearing a cardigan sweater a few seats away casually asked him what the date was and he had acidly replied, "Now, I have to give a class on the calendar."

Hennessey wore the kind of ragged mustache and general scowl that one often sees in civil-war photographs. He sported a dingy blue uniform and had a watch with multiple dials, also showing the time in London and Tokyo. A small leather valise was slung from his shoulder for receipts and a brass coin changer and set of keys were suspended across his drooping midsection. He had a gendarme cap, with faded circular stripes, and a lapel pin with the utility name in some exotic script.

He was the only conductor who stood out among the several different trains coming home. There were various shapes of ticket punches, each a kind of signature of the man who made it. By the time the ticket was finished, half would be Hennessey's familiar lightning bolt, while the rest would be an odd assortment which I couldn't help but associate with actual objects; a kite, a fan, a space capsule, a bishop's miter, an anvil, a star, a slanted cross. To see one of those spent fares with such images almost seemed to transform it into a kind of tarot card, some arcane representation of my life.

As soon as Hennessey entered the car, he would drone "Have your tickets ready. Don't be shy." I admit that there were mornings when, ensconced in a magazine or carried off by some reverie, I was a little late in displaying my token. In the depths of my wallet, there was always a profusion of cards and scribbled notes to wade through: expired licenses, reminders to call so and so. The wait couldn't have delayed him more than a few seconds. Nevertheless, he would always stick his hand toward you in a peremptory way and rub his fingers together in that crass, twitchy gesture, which used to signify "pay up."

No doubt he had his troubles like anyone else and perhaps the falling stock market had forced him to push his retirement back a few years. Maybe extra cars had been added or locomotive personnel had been pared by cutbacks. But I had seen other conductors who did not seem especially rushed and were even sometimes playful, such as when they would lean out the entrance at a sixty-degree angle from the handrails like Olympic ski jumpers.

Two months before, I had watched Hennessey rudely evict a woman who had obviously just forgotten her pocketbook and later I felt ashamed that I had not intervened on her behalf. One icy Monday, when due to a switching problem, the whole train had to be evacuated and herded onto buses, instead of being apologetic, he shoved a couple of passengers on his way to the microphone and acted as officious as a petty despot. He once accused me, with his catarrhal voice and accent I've never been able to place, of deliberately standing in the vestibule between cars to avoid payment. Before I located my right to be on the train, he gave me the option of getting off at the next stop or "doing jail time."

One nondescript day toward the end of Lent, again looking out the window, I noticed a sign featuring a racetrack with a bunch of thoroughbreds tearing down the stretch, while a lone jockey sped the opposite way. The banner underneath read, "Sure you're going the right direction?" It was another securities firm trying to pretend it knew the future, but they only managed to highlight my predicament. A short, listless woman in her fifties must have been unfamiliar with the routine and had to purchase her single voucher on the spot.

"Where did you get on?" Hennessey asked, in the censorious tone he reserved for those who had bypassed the station agent. A bit startled by his looming bulk, she hesitated. "Where did you get on?" he repeated, enunciating the last word so emphatically that he seemed to momentarily lose his balance.

"Downtown," she said, clearly flustered. "I'm going to the Ogilvie Center. The one with the lion statues at the entrance."

Now, he was glaring down at her imperiously, "I know where you get off. That's where the whole train is headed." It was then that he began yelling and his face began to show mottled patches, little veins at his temples coming into wavy relief. "Where did you get on? On?" Of course, none of the monthly ticket holders, flashing them like badges, moved a muscle in her defense. Someone in uniform, no matter how idiotic, always had the edge, the home-field advantage. It was no different than the world at large.

I almost took a swing at him that time but saw Terry Westbrook, a guy with whom I had butted heads over a parking place, with his ever-present *Wall Street Journal*. I didn't want to give him the satisfaction of watching me be led away by the policeman at the terminal, allow the misadventures to be the leading party talk with his racket club crowd. He would embellish it like a joke on a cocktail napkin, have it that I was smashed and wearing pajamas beneath my coat. He would have the neighborhood whispering that they knew something like that would happen after Libby left. When Hennessey kept up the cross examination, and she'd gone blank under the assault, I said I'd seen her get on at Central Street and handed him a fin.

In early April, the bite of winter was beginning to wane, and there were a few harbingers of Spring; the soft, muddy earth re-emerging, rabbits pausing on lawns to sniff the air. I had plunged into some paperwork about designs of various Roman goddesses being tested for a new line of women's tennis gear. The train was suffused with the dank residue of an ocean of puddles.

"Well, hello" Magdelena said, with the reticence of fragile associations, apparently not sure I would remember her. It took me a second to extract myself from the pantheon but my smile was automatic and I asked, "Have you been getting enough sleep these days?"

"Oh, not always, but I've sworn off those pills for good. I wondered if I would ever run into you again." She seemed relieved I'd recognized her and went on to explain that she had finished filling in on another shift for a coworker who had been pregnant and was now back on her former schedule. It seemed like the sort of second chance one almost never gets in life. She was surely as striking as the figures of Venus, Juno, and Minerva I had been wading through.

She sat down and immediately there was the same wonderful scent mixed with a trace of rain. I could hardly believe my luck, even as my mind raced ahead to how I could ask for her number. She began talking about the difference between the early and late hours when Hennessey strode vigilantly down the aisle. I checked my ticket and saw that there were two fares left. When he drew even with our seat, he assumed his usual demeanor, acknowledging Magdelena's weekly pass. With a cursory review of my own, he started punching a succession of gouges to void it like a volley of machine gun fire. In a voice full of weariness and false authority, he stated, "Last one," and jammed it into his pouch.

You might have thought that under the circumstances I would have swallowed my indignation at Hennessey's surly myopia and taken the three-dollar loss, but my forbearance was at an end. In an incredulous manner, I shouted, "No it isn't." He fixed me with a baleful stare and looked like he might reach for his walkie-talkie. Instead, he dug into his sack and handed the card back, crumpled and half torn to pieces.

"I've got a whole train to check buddy," Hennessey barked, his jaw tightening like a vice. "You find those invisible rides, and I'll be back."

Magdelena sat motionless beside me as the whole car turned its attention to the disturbance. She began searching her purse, maybe out of an urge to hide her face or perhaps for a weapon her detective books had prompted her to carry. The ticket had been fairly obliterated by Hennessey's zigzag holes interspersed with the kites and balloons and chess pieces, so that the remaining ride was gone. It came to me that when Libby had stormed out on that final night, she had broken some things of mine; pictures, souvenirs from faraway places, little things but of the sort you could never get back again. The thought somehow led from one affront to the next and recalled her malign prophecy.

I could hear the syncopation of the rails and as Hennessey proceeded through the car, I felt some insensate emotion arise within me. If he had been closer, I might have lunged and grabbed him by his ludicrous lapels. As it was, in the nuclear fury of the moment, I could not bear to shift and gauge Magdelena's reaction. I stood up and shouted with all the primal force in my being, "That was not the last one!"

The judgment from our audience in that humid atmosphere was etched indelibly in their harsh gaze and derisive laughter. I was momentarily shocked how reflexively they had sided with such an ignoramus, how fast they turned into a mob. After a moment in which Hennessey hissed something into his receiver, I could sense other uniformed men sounding the alarm and it was only then I noticed that Magdelena, this beautiful stranger, was no longer beside me. I spun only to see the last of her brilliant floral scarf disappear into the vestibule. It may have been a mirage, but through the murky oval glass, I thought she turned for an instant, with a look not of scorn, but of warmth and tenderness. Inside the careening train, with several conversations merging in a jumble and lights from a thousand anonymous sources punctuating the dark, I was almost sure of it.

## *House Crawl*

When the Naughtons moved to Spirit Island Estates, it was one of those decisions that looked like a sure thing, a natural path, so alluring in its possibilities as to seem irresistible. With Reed's company losing big accounts to the Pacific rim, his boss had begun hovering like a killer drone. One need not look further than the ashtray on the tiny patio outside the breakroom, the way the partially smoked, stubbed-out cigarettes stood in a skewed cluster—pillars of some primeval ruin—to sense there was trouble. In the gritty office of an Oil Change Express, Greta read an article about how people in the U.S. replaced their friends on average about every seven years. For some reason, it appeared they had begun to fit the mold. People they once saw on a fairly regular basis began to hide behind their email and Facebook accounts. Caller ID seemed increasingly a security system and their families were scattered across the country like explorers. One afternoon the idea seized them that they were on the wrong road, heading in a direction which led nowhere, that they had better throw out the old map and start from scratch.

The Island, as it was usually called, was a new colony where one could buy a spacious Dutch Revival for a couple hundred grand. The community was pleasantly separate from the fractious effects of the city, in an area that sported three small lakes and a private golf course. It had a corridor of free space that ran behind most of the backyards and also featured a security entrance, framed by a limestone arch that had the grandeur of some famous portal, to keep the chaos of the wide world at bay. Reed and Greta couldn't even have said exactly what they wanted—something less compressed, away from the bungalows and accidents of proximity they'd grown up with, yet not too far. They were both able to secure jobs, she as a bookkeeper for a carpet company, he as a supplier of machine parts, which seemed a modest upgrade from their former grind. Their five-year-old son, Otis, would no longer be bouncing off the walls of a bedroom whose cramped dimensions reminded them of an attic.

Reed sat with Brian Trent after their round of golf at the Arrowhead Grill, lounging under an umbrella with some Italian logo, now and then glancing at the shots that bounded up toward the 18th green. The hole's flag would lift slightly and fall, catching subtle fluctuations of the wind. The panorama seemed to extend for miles, without a shopping mall or office building to blight the natural contour. The other players had already departed for various errands, but the two men lingered partly because all the manicured grass, with its quiet order, represented a kind of sanctuary.

"You would have had a good back nine except for the 16th," Brian said, adding the series of numbers on the score card. Reed vividly remembered his drive striking the famous "cleavage tree" on the edge of the 16th fairway, so named for its two large symmetrical humps next to one another, like a goddess on the prow of a Viking ship. The ball had caromed out of bounds and across the street into the Micelli's tomato plants.

"It's a good omen hitting that tree though," Brian said with his characteristically sanguine take on things. "Don't be surprised if you get lucky tonight."

"It would be nice, but I don't think Greta's very susceptible to tree magic," Reed said, rolling his eyes.

"Just one of the nutty local legends, but for your sake I hope it's true."

Brian and girlfriend Mandy lived two doors down and had helped to anchor the Naughtons, almost acting like sponsors at an exclusive club. Brian had just the right amount of sociability, which was neither remote nor prying, and a similar addiction to summer sports. He had the smallest handwriting Reed had ever seen, very precise, a signature that required a magnifying glass and a tendency to deftly change the subject if things got awkward, never cutting you off, often summoning some odd item from the internet as a kind of detour. He was moderately successful, having gotten in early on the tanning salon craze and seemed one of those guys who is a little clairvoyant, who could spot the next big thing before the rest of the herd. Greta had also taken to Mandy right away, having met her at a Photoshop class taught in the community house.

"What do you make of people shooting at the menhirs?" Reed asked, recalling the weekend's news. "Didn't we all move out here to get away from this kind of stuff?"

The signature element of the development's theme was the "menhirs," rough stone monoliths about seven feet high supposedly excavated from a site somewhere in the county, artifacts of a tribe that had flourished millennia before. There were a few of them, all with some crude markings, placed at strategic locations throughout the settlement. No doubt they had once been a boon to the village's marketing scheme, but lately a certain faction had objected to how they tied up parcels of land, even hinting they were somehow heathen and apocalyptic. One menhir had recently been vandalized to depict a rather menacing alien figure with the caption, "They are coming!"

This crime might have been dismissed as part of the overall graffiti problem if it weren't for someone who was obviously using some of the menhirs for target practice. At first, people mistook the popping sounds in the wee hours for fireworks or vehicle backfires, but it became obvious the stones were becoming embedded with the fragments of bullets.

"Well, a few folks are upset," Brian said, his line of sight still out along the fairway. "Those boulders are some kind of focal point. They seem to be in the way of some other things. I don't think it's much to worry about." He seemed briefly distracted when a group of women on the other side of the deck broke into a collective paroxysm of laughter that had them nearly gasping for oxygen.

"Bullets flying around are something to worry about in my view," Reed said, regretting the sense of complaint that had crept into his voice.

"I guess there's some issue about running lines for cable in the same areas, that it's some kind of sacrilege. That the routers are an eyesore and all that. But people will fight for their TV. It's their lifeline to civilization." Brian still had his sunglasses on, so Reed couldn't tell if he cared one way or the other.

Reed had to admit that it sometimes felt like they had been banished to some outpost at the ends of the earth. Radios and cell phones would fade in and out, surrounded by a void of static. An antenna signal decoder had to be positioned just right, the blinds drawn, and the bric a brac on the mantle arranged just so or the digital picture would dissolve into an incomprehensible array of pixels. Reed had noticed a few of the router boxes rising up out of the ground in some of the common areas. They had dull oblong frames with columns of jittery dials, emitting a perpetual low whir with blinking red lights set close enough together that it wasn't hard to imagine them as a pair of eyes.

Later in the locker room, Reed overheard some joking with Brian about a woman other than Mandy. When Reed asked him about it, Brian became preoccupied as though he'd misplaced a shirt in his duffle bag, and said, "Things are sort of in a state of flux." They left separately but from the opposite side of the lot, Reed saw Brian get into a tank-like van that was not his own, a woman he'd never seen at the wheel. It was none of Reed's business, so he decided not to wave as the driver eased the two of them, quickly immersed in each other's company, out into the trafficless street.

Reed was often grateful for Greta's social elan; without her he'd probably be forced to join some sad alliance of misfits. Yet after the initial excitement of a new home slowly faded, she began to withdraw more and more into her photography. When she took a picture of some ordinary thing, a park bench or a plastic flamingo on someone's lawn, keenly twisting her lens as if she were capturing the pyramids, he couldn't help but feel her passion was misplaced. It seemed every few months Greta would receive a condescending letter conveying that she had not won a contest, offering her some pathetic consolation like a discount on digital batteries. Though she did a valiant job of hiding her setbacks, a few times he caught her rereading the notifications, as if the words might somehow reconfigure themselves in her favor. Once in an attempt to bolster her mood, he said, "Don't get upset honey. It's all fixed anyway. As fixed as a fortune teller at a traveling circus."

There was a time when she would have felt lifted by this concern, but lately such a remark would devolve into a ritual argument about how Reed was too downbeat. His sense of the paths to disaster in almost any situation, accrued over a decade now, had shredded her innate sense of optimism. She once said that Reed's glass was not half full but barely contained a few drops. It didn't help that Otis had become a skilled mimic and appeared to be picking up some of his vices. The other day, after grabbing a coloring book, Otis had asked "Where's the damn pencil?" as heedlessly as a longshoreman.

Greta kept remarking about Mandy's blog, a hobby of hers, pressing him to read her last post, though by and large Reed shied away from the internet's distractions. He had seen countless others get drawn into the web's glowing vortex, devouring whole pieces of their lives, as insidious as the Indian casino in Broadport. He might have offered an excuse if the writer hadn't been Mandy, who held for him some elusive intrigue. She was a tall, sandy blond, with an eye-catching walk and an air of preoccupation. With a child from a former marriage, she freelanced articles from home on a wide array of topics she often knew little about beforehand. Reed was drawn to her reserve, which seemed to mask an appraising intelligence, and tended to cause others to talk about their situations more than they otherwise might.

One Saturday morning, Reed came across Greta's website. There was a motto at the top that read: "Smallgripes.com—Shining a light on mankind's little annoyances since 2006." Beside this there was a vaguely-sketched woman with the look of a gorgon, hair sticking out in all directions and eyes ablaze, with what appeared like steam coming out of her head. Mandy's dissatisfactions apparently ran the gamut. The first few topics in the index were:

    -people who pretend they're unaware you're behind them.

- dramas with the obligatory torture scene
- ripped out articles in magazines at the doctor's office
- the substitution of "yep" for "you're welcome"
- marketing: the new hypnotism
- the euphemistic style of waiters

This last entry began, "Does it bother anyone else that for as long as I can remember every waiter and waitress in America uses the same standard phrase for determining if she/he should remove your plate from the table? We all know what they say, without variation, no matter what their ethnic background, no matter whether you're eating goat in the Addis Ababa Cafe or pancakes at the local diner, whether their inflection is gentle or matter of fact or brusque. They say, "Are you still working on that?" This question is obviously a code the restaurant owners everywhere seem to impose on their staffs: a mantra, a forced expression, a euphemism, for determining when the customer is finished. Doesn't this rob the server of any originality whatsoever? And aren't we all sick to death of it?"

There were dozens of other pieces like that, most with messages of approval from her readers in smaller script. She had even scored an advertiser, a local florist who was offering a discount on the flower of the month. It struck him that Mandy had never outwardly betrayed a hint of frustration or sarcasm, nothing to suggest some smoldering critic. In person, Reed could not recall her declaring a single grievance. Her demeanor was usually so composed, as if she were on another plane of existence that somehow skimmed above the fray. It was a not unpleasant shock that like him, she found so much to fault. She suddenly seemed one of those women who always kept something hidden, some aspect that was always out of reach. This was not to mention the attractive, not too conspicuous swale of her hips.

The following week, when Greta was at the allergist, Reed got off early to pick up Otis from his playdate with Mandy's son Paul. Reed had seen Mandy dozens of times by then, but it was always in their foursomes with Brian holding court. With the likelihood that he wouldn't be there, Reed just wanted to conceal his mild crush and get through this exercise with a minimum of awkwardness. He was a bit startled when Paul opened the door holding one of the Otis's squirt guns and wearing a zombie mask.

"Aren't you a little young to want to eat other people?" Reed asked him.

"Mom's in the back," he replied impatiently, before dashing down a set of stairs to where Otis was probably immersed in a mountain of toys. Reed looked up to see Mandy on the small terrace leaning over her laptop, beyond which lay a modest inflatable pool. He maneuvered his way through a sliding door.

"Sorry, my deadline's tomorrow," she said, half getting up, now that the spell of continuity had been broken. Her eyes rested on his for a fleeting second before darting toward the interior of the house. "I hope Greta's okay."

"She's fine. Just a little routine maintenance."

"Let me see if the demolition crew is ready to come up."

As she moved past him, in her jeans and untucked blouse, he couldn't help but notice that she was pretty in a different way than Greta. Her walk was subtly more of a swaying motion, her arms swinging a bit more freely. And there was a slight measure of self-consciousness in her movements he found unexpectedly sexy. Reed had never really asked her about the blog, never told her he found her observations clever and biting. He wondered if one of his own idiosyncrasies, his habit of grabbing his left ear when things got uncomfortable, would be mentioned in a future installment. But he couldn't imagine when he might ever broach the subject, certainly not then with the kids within earshot, and just wanted to manage an uncomplicated exit.

When the boys came up, Otis sported nearly the full array of his arsenal: handcuffs, blaster, vampire claws, night binoculars, and light saber. Reed remembered an episode from the previous night when he had made a mess of repairing the tangled lines of a Captain America parachute. It was an epic display of manual ineptitude, and Otis had said, "You're a good father but a terrible assistant."

"Hey dad," Otis said nonchalantly, somehow a combination of relief that he had not been abandoned and regret that he was being tugged back into the mundane world.

"Make sure he comes back soon, Reed," Mandy said, "as long as they leave the house still standing." Reed was watching Paul and Otis signal their bashful goodbyes, and when he turned, he was struck by the way Mandy was resting her arm against the jamb and the enigma of her smile, so that he could only shout, "Sure" nearly stumbling as he turned toward the car.

The weather could not have been better for the annual House Crawl, on an unusually warm October night. Illuminated balls could be seen zooming across the sky, heralding the end of the night-golf tournament, which kicked off the procession. Revelers advanced in a string of golf carts like some carnival ride, bearing dozens of conversations and cocktails in their sinuous wake. Some were armed with flashlights as if ready to form a search party if one of their wayward number should stray from the circuit.

At the first house, the Scanlon living room was scattered with momentos of intrepid exploits. There were photographs of astronauts, maps of the route around Cape Horn, and a whole shelf devoted to the hunt for the source of the Nile. Yet there was scant respect shown for their little museum. Shelly Moreno received an ovation for balancing a Turkish vase on her head for thirty seconds, and George Nix did a wobbly handstand before tipping over into a bust of Magellan.

As people migrated outside, Greta vanished with a group of women Reed barely recognized, though he could hear some of them cavorting to an 80's dance number on the back porch. He spotted Brian hamming it up across the lawn about one of the council votes. Mandy wasn't with him, possibly drawn elsewhere by the random eddies of the crowd.

Bill Hettinger, the real estate agent who had reeled them in, briefly rested a huge arm on Reed's shoulder, and peered into a picture window. "How's everything, buddy? I love these things. Getting inside all these houses to see what they're worth. Eliminates the guesswork." Hettinger moved his cigarette around in quick bursts, unable to contain his nervous energy.

"Yeah, I know what you mean," Reed responded, forcing himself to grin, though he didn't understand half of what Bill said about the business. He remembered that right after their purchase, when Bill had taken them out to dinner in a sports car, they imagined him losing control and flipping end over end.

"I heard our pal Brian has gone off the reservation. No open house there," Bill said, in his best conspiratorial whisper.

"How's that exactly?" Reed asked, just as Brian spied him and signaled, raising his glass.

"He's got a little action going on the side. Apparently they don't agree about that business with the stones, and Brian is in pretty deep . . . . Too bad. Mandy's a nice gal. I sold her that big lot in '98."

Reed wasn't shocked at this disclosure exactly, yet it was still hard to incorporate what he had just heard with his image of Brian. The information felt like magnets whose force naturally repelled each other, impossible to merge. Then someone hailed Bill from an overstuffed cart already in humming motion, so that he abruptly excused himself, trotted over and jumped in the back like a caddy.

The restless contingent meandered to two or three more bacchanals, leaving a trail of half-eaten appetizers and melting ice cubes. All the dwellings seemed to have only minor design variations, lending a false sense of familiarity. But the pattern was interrupted when they arrived at Rex Hartrich's enormous pontoon houseboat, which might have been mistaken for a ferry. Every year someone managed to fall in, but there had never been a drowning or a police report, so when such an accident inevitably happened, it took on the character of a prehistoric custom. Reed and Greta paused at the base of the dock, where Hartrich had rigged up a tent to accommodate the overflow, and made themselves a drink.

"Maybe we should bring a small scuba tank just in case?" Reed said, as he studied Rex farther down the pier, dressed like an admiral.

Greta ignored the remark, sweeping some windblown curls out of her vision, which, with her long, flowing hair seemed almost a compulsive gesture. It had already been a rough day. Greta had gotten a call from Monica Remick in the old neighborhood asking them back for a birthday barbecue. She said she practically had to hire a detective to track down their whereabouts. This invite seemed to erase all the feuds that sometimes plagued them before, and filled Greta with a burst of nostalgia. But there was a maze of obstacles—a playdate scheduled for weeks, Otis's baseball practice, tickets to see *Barefoot in the Park* at the summer stock theatre— so they had to pass.

Their commutes had become a war of attrition, half of it on crumbling State Highway 9, whose gaping fissures tested their axels on a daily basis. That morning Greta had hit a bump that, in her words, "seemed to lift the whole chassis off the ground and send me into low orbit." Later, when Reed made a playful remark about the den was starting to look like a "dust farm," Greta began throwing things. She indiscriminately reached for any nonlethal object that could be rendered airborne: magazines, couch pillows, the occasional paperback novel, then finally a bunch of bananas. These were not lobbed but hurled full force as a primitive might repel an invader, crashing into the shelves behind him. Reed, never violent by nature, merely ducked and weaved and protected his head until her fury was spent.

Now, Greta checked her purse, no doubt making sure the camera was there in case an interesting set of lines or buoys presented themselves in the proper light. "This should be fun. I just loved Uncle Steve's catamaran when I was a kid."

"Would that be the Uncle Steve who accepted a plea bargain for tax fraud?"

Greta shot him one of her signature looks of annoyance that he understood was a warning to leave her family alone.

Rex greeted everyone effusively like he was the concierge of a cruise ship and handed each guest a miniature telescope. He loved the vessel dearly. The joke was that Rex's will directed his body be placed in the bow, with the craft pointed toward the middle of the lake and set ablaze.

They boarded gingerly, reckoning with the principles of balance, and scanned the boat for someone they knew. The dimensions of the main deck were about the same as a boxing ring and a sign said that at 11 p.m. the area was reserved as a dance floor. Reed took Greta's hand so that they could shift and squeeze their way to the corner. Reed always felt better with a drink in his hand, but with the press of bodies and subtle shifts in the current, not spilling it required all his concentration, as if he were crossing a high wire. Greta spotted Gwen Meeks who beckoned them from the far railing.

They talked a while over the rhythmic Sinatra tunes, covering a string of the hamlet's oddities. There was the recent encroachment of coyotes, with a few of them brazenly venturing down Main Street and across the tennis courts. Members of the Masonic Theosophical Society were threatening litigation over a new logo. The bird club was in a dispute over whether a rare Pileated Woodpecker had been spotted near the Ashburns' greenhouse. But most of the stories seemed to center around the menhirs.

Ruth Bennett was convinced that they were responsible for the remission of her lymphoma. Every Saturday morning, she laid flowers or some other offering at the base of the one nearest her duplex. An archeology professor from the community college weighed in saying the tribe that had constructed them was nomadic and held ceremonies to figure out which way to head next. When a router had been installed in one of the clearings where a couple of menhirs stood, the history faction seemed to gather strength. A few gear boxes had been ripped off and scattered. Homes in that section found just a snowy nothingness on the TV where a ballgame or a reality show should have been.

There was a big splash on the port side, and a woman yelled in a theatrical, panicked voice, "Man overboard!" Hartrich sounded a tinny alarm. A roar went up when the boat tilted slightly in the lake as people rushed to get a view. Reed only caught a glimpse, but it was clear that whole thing had been staged as Dale Haney, buoyed by giant life preserver, held his bourbon aloft like a trophy.

A minute later, two guys near the boarding ramp began arguing about the cable boxes. A barrage of insults and some shoving followed, and Reed overheard a woman say she'd seen a flash of a holstered gun. Then, Brian appeared out of nowhere, speaking in a tense but familiar manner, and the conflict died down as suddenly as it erupted. Reed started across a seam in the huddling crowd to say hello just as the wake from a distant runabout sent him lurching against a set of ropes.

"Hey, stop rocking the boat," Brian said, with a mock serious expression, his companions having dispersed.

"And here I thought it was the other way around," Reed said, closer to the truth than he intended. "I don't want to fall in. I hear they've stocked the lake with man-eating sharks. Another sales gimmick."

"Don't worry. We have plenty of harpoons."

"Where's Mandy?" Reed said, knowing he shouldn't but unable to resist. "A trove of blog material here, I would think."

"You've read it?"

"Greta showed it to me once or twice," he said, trying not to seem too interested. "She's very good." Reed thought of what withering reflections she might acquire from an event like this, though maybe she had to keep certain things off limits, and cover her tracks. He couldn't help the feeling that in the manner they apprehended the world, the two of them were somehow matched.

"Maybe a little too good sometimes," Brian said, quickly looking out in the direction of the marina. "She's a regular spy." His face changed in the aquatic, shadowy light, and for the first time since Reed had known him, Brian's bonhomie failed, as his mouth briefly twisted into a shape of malice. It was as if some façade had been broken, altering the whole texture of things, the entire setting taking on the quality of an illusion.

Summoned by another acquaintance, Brian excused himself and disappeared behind a group of dancers as effectively as if a curtain had been drawn. Reed wanted to talk to Greta, find a pretext to leave, but he couldn't see her now and figured she might have gone with a group that had talked about a stroll down the beach. Deciding not to search for her, he made his way beyond the canted row of masts in the harbor. The cavalcade of carts was still lined along the dirt hill leading down to the jetty. He walked up a rise and glanced back at diminutive Spirit Island resting only a thousand yards from shore, an uninhabited place with a single wharf and lookout tower, which to him always had the feel of desertion. He veered along the edge of the empty course and noticed a faint light farther into the trees where it didn't seem there should have been one. It was a moonless night and off the beaten path, the features of the land, the drop-offs, were barely visible.

Just as he paused to consider whether it was worth investigating, he saw someone strolling about fifty yards down the lake road. He decided it wasn't time to trek back to the others and pulled out his cell so whoever it was wouldn't be startled.

"Hey," a woman called out weakly, as if she had been a little frightened nevertheless. He recognized it was Mandy from the voice, some octave that alone belonged to her, before she fully emerged along the gravel shoulder.

"It's just Reed," he said, figuring she hadn't made out his face yet as she stood, neither advancing nor retreating. He had instinctively inserted the word "just" to emphasize his harmlessness with no one else around but the greeting felt strangely apt, one perhaps to use as a standard introduction.

"Reed," she half shouted, after an audible sigh. "I can't tell you how glad I am that you're not the Boston Strangler."

"We seem to have wandered away from the caravan." He could see now that she was smoking a cigarette and speculated that she had wanted to do that far from the reproach of her neighbors. She looked wonderful in her tight calf-length skirt and strapped sandals, yet something in her sagging posture seemed to disdain all the frivolity.

"I'm afraid I've missed most of the party. Sometimes you get the feeling you've seen it all before."

"I was just trying to decide whether to check out a strange phenomenon," he said, avoiding his own reasons for leaving the boat, trying to suppress the buoyant sensation of being secluded with an attractive woman, the pleasant danger. He wondered whether the rumor of Brian having an affair were true and if he might discern through the angle of her stance, which now featured one knee slightly pushing out the material, whether she knew. He could count the times he had exclusively talked to Mandy on one hand, but because of the blog, he almost felt like they were keepers of a secret pact.

"Really, I'm afraid to ask what but I will anyway."

"Over there. That can't be a spotlight."

"I see what you mean. Maybe we should wait for reinforcements."

"Sorry, I can't help myself. If you see any spaceships materialize, head back to camp."

Reed slowly crept down the mild grade into the acacia and weeping willows trees and into a small clearing that hadn't been apparent from the street. He saw immediately what it was. A few of the glowballs had been so errant at that bend of the dogleg that they had gone out of bounds, over a chain link fence and settled, pooling their fluorescence. It was only when he stepped closer to retrieve them, souvenirs of his little expedition, that he made out the menhir, rising like a mute witness. Mandy had followed him without his hearing, and when he turned she stood just a few feet away, staring at the graven image. She had recently written a piece, about how they represented a kind of sacredness, a rare sense of permanence.

"They always seem to turn up when you least expect it," she said, edging a little closer, with only the sound of the long grass. "At least for now. Until they quietly disappear."

"Is it really like that?" Reed said, inspecting the rough shape, its etching mostly obscured. Something made him think of Greta, whether she was wondering where he was, even though people were always losing each other on the House Crawl. He still loved Greta, but he could no longer

133

remember a time when there wasn't some impenetrable fabric of strife stretched between them, a line of demarcation neither could cross.

"Which side are you on?" Mandy asked playfully, as if it didn't mean anything. "The past or the future?"

"I guess I'm still working on that."

Under the soft sky, a mild breeze barely stirring the branches, a thrumming charge seemed to fill him, slowly at first, and then more insistently, the kind of release he felt when the whiskey started to change the composition of his blood. There was a moment when they just stood close, waiting to be hurled one way or another. Then somehow they were down on the edge of the knoll, leaves bristling under their sudden weight, entwined like it were some instinct of survival, as if the weight of their disenchantment would otherwise crush them.

Perhaps it was the shots which punctuated the darkness, neither close nor very far, that acted like a kind of admonition and made them draw back. It entered into Reed's mind that someone was shooting at the menhir, and oddly, when the impression came to mind, it was Brian pulling the trigger, dressed in camouflage gear, chuckling with every hunk of the thing that was gouged off. But soon the reports stopped and no one else was there.

They rose from the ground and began drifting back toward the clamor of the revelry. "It must be our celebrated spirits," Reed said, as they gathered themselves. But the look that passed across Mandy's face, amid the spectral traces of light, seemed unsure whether he meant the kiss or the gunfire. Then there was the sound of the carts' engines rumbling, the raucous convoy once again on the move.

# *Home and Castle*
# by
# Thomas Benz

**Winner of the 2017 Serena McDonald Kennedy Fiction Award**

### *Previous Winners*

| | | |
|---|---|---|
| Dwight Yates | *Haywire Hearts and Slide Trombones* | 2006 |
| Brian Bedard | *Grieving on the Run* | 2007 |
| Kathy Flann | *Smoky Ordinary* | 2008 |
| Wendy Marcus | *Polyglot* | 2009 |
| Starkey Flythe | *Driving With Hand Controls* | 2010 |
| Richard Fellinger | *They Hover Over Us* | 2011 |
| Dwight Holing | *California Works* | 2012 |
| John Zeugner | *Under Hiroshima, Collected Stories* | 2013 |
| Jacob M. Appel | *The Magic Laundry* | 2014 |
| Misty Urban | *A Lesson in Manners* | 2015 |
| Patricia O'Donnell | *Gods for Sale* | 2016 |

# Serena McDonald Kennedy

Serena McDonald Kennedy was born in 1850 on the fourth of July. She was the fifth of seven daughters and the ninth of 12 children, of James and Serena Swain McDonald in Thomas County, Georgia. She was descended from Alexander McDonald, a Scottish Highlander, who fought with General James Oglethorpe at the Battle of Bloody Marsh, which saved Florida from the Spanish. His son was our Revolutionary hero.

Her father and mother, after marriage, settled on a farm between the McDonald and Swain plantations, later occupying the Reese plantation and finally the Swain plantation where they lived until their deaths. A town grew up around their home site named McDonald, Georgia, now known as Pavo, making James one of the first real estate developers of the area.

Serena, although far down the list of girls, had her mother's name, one, it was said, that fit her personality. Only a few years after her birth, her father would go to war as a Lieutenant-Colonel in the Confederacy, and she would lose a brother in the War Between the States. We have in our possession a long letter written in beautiful Spencerian script from her brother, Kenneth, a Captain, on April 20, 1863 (when she was 13 and he was 23), from "near Fredricksburg, Virgina." He wrote of the beauty of Spring: *"The weather has turned warm and pleasant at last. The cold icy blast of winter has past and all nature looks revived. The sufferings of a cold hard winter seem to have been all forgotten and a few warm days have induced the trees to put forth their Buds and Blossoms. Everything seems to be in a high state of pleasure and glee. Everything is beautiful and harmonious. It's a bright Sabbath morning.* And as a postscript, he wrote: *"You will excuse this miserable bad written thing of a letter; for God's sake don't show it."* Only two weeks later, he was wounded at Chancellorsville and died three weeks later.

At 35, Serena was what was then generally called "an old maid," who came to the community of Enon in Thomas County as a school teacher. There she met and married John Thomas Kennedy, ten years her junior. Tom, as he was called, had lost a young wife and child in childbirth, and he and Serena began a life together that lasted for 40 years, until Serena died at the age of 75. Tom died 10 years later. They were the parents of four children, the second of whom was my father, Archibald Randolph Kennedy.

My grandmother was a great believer in education, and to our ultimate benefit, she saw that my father went to prep school and college, unusual in the rural area in which our family lived. His education influenced our family in many ways, and I attribute my love of literature to that heritage.

Although Serena died before I was born, my mother, Adeline Kennedy, was so devoted to her mother-in-law that she quoted her often and patterned our development after what she learned from her mother-in-law. My sister, Martha Stephenson, my brother, William Kennedy, and I are her only grandchildren living today. It is a great honor for us to have the Serena McDonald Kennedy Award named for her.

Barbara Kennedy Passmore

# Snake Nation Press Supporters

Barbara Passmore & The Price-Campbell Foundation
The Porter-Fleming Foundation
The Georgia Council for the Arts
Gloria & Wilby Coleman
Dr. Manual Tovar
Lowndes/Valdosta Arts Commission
Cynthia Schumacher in memory of
L. H. St. John
James Najarian in Memoriam: Robin Najarian
Don Hoffman & Sue Hellstern
Dean Poling & *The Valdosta Daily Times*
Morris Smith and the Smith Family
Robin Pennington and Autumn Pennington in memory of their Mother, Vicki Pennington
June Purvis in memory of Dr. Jerry Purvis
Our Subscribers

## *South Georgia Literacy Festival Supporters*

JL Concepts
Michael and Martha Dover
Citizens Community Bank
John's Body Shop
Joanna Bridges
Willis Miller
First Federal Savings and Loan
F. L. Wilson
Valdosta Teachers Federal Credit Union
FVSC Valdosta Area Alumni Chapter